He leaned down a plant a rough, hard kiss on her mouth....

Lucia was lost as soon as he touched her. When, finally, he let her go, the world had changed and would never be the same again. Trembling, breathless, dizzy, amazed, Lucia stayed where she was while Grey stepped back a pace.

"I didn't intend it to happen," he said, his voice thick.

She could think of nothing to say. All she wanted was to be back in his arms.

"You said you wanted some tea," he reminded her. He moved away.

Lucia was astonished he could function normally. She still felt like someone in shock. Surely it couldn't be his intention to behave as if nothing had happened?

"Grey...." she began huskily, what she wanted to say eluding her but knowing something must be said. They couldn't possibly go back to the way they had been before.

"Yes?"

She braced herself. "Why did you do it?"

Dear Reader,

This story is special. It marks the forty-fifth anniversary of the publication of *Winter is Past*, my first romance—way back in 1955.

In the 1950s I was in my twenties, a newspaper reporter. My first seven books were written in my spare time. Then, with my thirtieth birthday on the horizon, I gave up staff journalism to start a family. The heroine of *A Call for Nurse Templar* was a midwife, and the story was inspired by my experience of having a baby at home rather than in hospital as is more usual today. After that I became a full-time writer. But, until 1978 when my son set off on the first of his many adventures, I adapted my working hours to suit the equally important responsibilities of being a wife and mother.

Most of my stories had exotic backgrounds. Although I still love to travel, nowadays some of my most exciting journeys take place in cyberspace. At six o'clock every morning I log on to the Internet, picking up e-mails from colleagues around the world and looking for Web sites to do with my favorite relaxation—reading.

Over the years I've had letters from readers in Africa, America, Australia, India and all parts of Europe. Lately, however, instead of these heartwarming letters being delivered by the postman, they are starting to pop into the mailbox on my computer.

If, when you finish this story, you have any comments, I shall enjoy hearing from you.

Anne Weale

WORTHY OF
MARRIAGE
Anne Weale

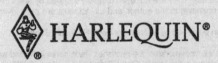

TORONTO • NEW YORK • LONDON
AMSTERDAM • PARIS • SYDNEY • HAMBURG
STOCKHOLM • ATHENS • TOKYO • MILAN • MADRID
PRAGUE • WARSAW • BUDAPEST • AUCKLAND

ISBN 0-373-03633-7

WORTHY OF MARRIAGE

First North American Publication 2000.

Visit us at www.eHarlequin.com

Printed in U.S.A.

CHAPTER ONE

ON THE morning of her release, Lucia Graham felt a mixture of exhilaration and dread.

She had been longing for freedom since the day she was sentenced to a year's imprisonment. As matters turned out she had not served the full term 'inside'. She was being allowed an early release.

But she knew that the world she was returning to would not be the world she had left. Now she had a prison record, and little chance of supporting herself in any congenial way. Who would want to employ a convicted criminal?

After she had changed into her own clothes—they smelt musty after so long in storage—she was taken to the office of the prison's deputy governor.

'You are bound to feel apprehensive, Graham,' said the older woman. 'Try to put the past behind you and make a completely fresh start. Easier said than done, I know, but fortunately there is someone who wants to help you rebuild your life.'

'Who?' Lucia asked bewilderedly.

'You will find that out shortly. A car is waiting outside. Goodbye and good luck.'

The deputy governor shook hands, making it clear she did not intend to explain her statement.

When, shortly afterwards, Lucia stepped through the wicket, an opening in one of the prison's massive double doors, she expected the car waiting for her to be a small saloon of the kind run by social workers. She couldn't think of anyone else who would want to help her.

There was only one car in the parking bay in front of the prison. It was an imposingly large and new-looking black limousine. As she stared at it, a uniformed driver got out and came towards her.

'Miss Lucia Graham?'

'Yes.'

'This way, please, miss.'

He led her towards the limousine and opened the rear offside passenger door, holding it for her as if she were someone respectable, not a jailbird.

About an hour later, after passing through a pretty village in an area that seemed to have escaped the urban development of much of southern England, the car entered the grounds of a large old house partially covered with Virginia creeper. Near the house the drive forked, one way leading round to the back of the building, the other opening into a large oval of gravel. Slowly, in order not to splatter the gravel on the surrounding lawn, the chauffeur drove in a half circle, bringing the car to a standstill a few yards from the front door.

About five minutes earlier, Lucia had seen him make a brief call on a mobile telephone. Evidently he had been notifying someone in the house of their arrival. As he opened the door for her, the front door opened and a woman appeared.

Stepping out of the car, Lucia thought at first that the stranger was in her late forties or early fifties. She was wearing a white shirt and blue denim skirt. A braided leather belt circled her slim waist. Her fair hair was brushed back from her forehead and cut in a classic bob. Her only make-up seemed to be lipstick.

'Miss Graham...welcome. My name is Rosemary.'
She held out her hand, taking Lucia's in a firm clasp.
'I'm sure you are longing for some coffee. Come in and
relax and I will explain the situation. You must be curious to know why you are here.'

After releasing Lucia's hand, she took her lightly by
the elbow to usher her into the house as if she were a
welcome guest.

As they entered a spacious hall dominated by a wide
flight of stairs with its lowest steps gracefully curved,
Lucia noticed at once that the walls were adorned with
numerous paintings.

So were the walls in the large drawing room where
coffee things were set out on a table near the open
French windows overlooking a terrace and a large well-
kept garden.

With a gesture inviting Lucia to seat herself in a comfortable armchair, Rosemary sat down in another and
reached for the tall china coffee pot.

'Miss Harris and I went to the same school,' she said,
referring to the prison governor. 'She is much younger
than I am. She was one of the new girls I had to take
under my wing when I was in my last year. We've met
and talked at several Old Girls' reunions. If she hadn't
known me, she might not have let me persuade her to
have you brought here.'

Lucia said nothing. Compared with the place she had
come from, this beautiful high-ceilinged room seemed
overwhelmingly luxurious. She felt as if she might be
dreaming and, at any moment, would wake up to find
it was all an illusion.

The other woman handed her a cup of fragrant coffee.
'Please help yourself to cream and sugar, if you take
them.'

It was then that Lucia realised Rosemary was older than she had thought. The front of the house had been in shade. Here in the south-facing drawing room, the mid-morning sunlight revealed a network of lines round her hostess's eyes and mouth. She was at least sixty-five.

'I won't keep you in suspense any longer,' said Rosemary, smiling at her. 'When I left school, I wanted to be an artist. During my first year at art college, I met my husband. He wanted me to concentrate on being a wife and mother. To please him—I was terribly in love—I let my ambitions go.'

She paused for a moment, obviously remembering the time when she had made that decision.

'Two years ago my husband died. Like most widows, I found it hard to adjust to living alone. I have four very dear children who are enormously supportive. But they have their own lives to lead. One of them thought I should start painting again. So I did. Now I need some-one to accompany me on painting trips abroad. I don't fancy going on my own. I thought you might like to come with me...as a combination of painting companion and private courier. How does the idea strike you?'

From her own point of view, it struck Lucia as a gift from the gods, but also as an act of madness on Rosemary's part.

'Why me?' she said.

'Because, as I understand it, you have nowhere to go, and you have the right qualifications. You're an accomplished painter and, equally importantly, a naturally caring person, as you proved by nursing your father so devotedly.'

Lucia stared at her, baffled. 'How can you trust me?' she asked.

'My dear, you were convicted of fraud...not murder. In my view it was unnecessarily harsh to send you to prison. There are situations in which any of us may be driven to acts quite foreign to our normal natures. You found yourself in one of those situations. What you did wasn't right...but it wasn't the kind of thing to put you beyond the pale of decent society. At least I don't think so.'

She had scarcely finished speaking when the door opened and they were joined by a tall, dark-haired man who would have been formally dressed in a city suit had he not taken off the coat, now slung over his arm, removed his tie and opened the collar of his shirt.

As he entered the room, his face showed the smiling expectation of someone sure of finding someone he liked there. This changed to surprise as he took in Lucia's presence. It was clear that he didn't recognise her.

She recognised him immediately. How could she ever forget him? This was the man who had played an important part in bringing her to trial and sending her to prison. His contemptuous glances as he stood in the witness box and she sat in the dock, listening to the evidence that had led to her conviction, had haunted her during the long, often sleepless nights in her cell.

'Oh...hello, darling...I wasn't expecting to see you today,' said Rosemary, looking slightly disconcerted. She turned to Lucia. 'This is my son Grey.' She introduced him as if they had no previous connection with each other. 'Grey, this is Lucia Graham.'

Clearly the name didn't ring a bell with him. At her trial, he had struck Lucia as a man with an excellent memory. But the day of their previous encounter had not been as important to him as to her. Once she had been dealt with, he had probably deleted her from his mental database.

Also she had looked different then. Her hair had been fashionably short and colour-rinsed. Now it was long and back to its natural light brown. She was thinner. Few people would recognise her as the young woman whose face had appeared in both the tabloid and broadsheet newspapers.

He came towards her.

Instinctively Lucia stood up, bracing herself for the moment when recognition dawned.

'How do you do?' He offered his hand.

She felt compelled to respond and to force a smile, but being friendly didn't feel right. So this was why Rosemary hadn't given her surname; knowing that, if she had, Lucia would have got to hell out of here.

After releasing her hand, Grey Calderwood turned his attention to his mother, stooping to brush a kiss on her cheek.

Straightening, he said, 'It's been a tough week. I felt like a day in the country.'

Someone else came into the room: a grey-haired woman in a plain blouse and skirt. She was carrying a cup and saucer. 'I saw you coming from upstairs, Mr Grey,' she said, smiling up at him.

'Thanks, Braddy.' He took the cup from her. As she was leaving, he filled it with coffee. 'I'm not interrupting anything, I hope?' The question was directed at both his mother and her guest. Then, to Lucia, he said, 'Mine being the only car outside, I take it you live locally, Ms Graham?'

'I hope Lucia is going to live here,' said Rosemary Calderwood. 'I've just offered her the job of being my painting partner.'

'Oh really?' Leaving the cup on the table, her son moved to the back of a nearby wing chair and pushed it closer to where they were sitting. As he sat down and crossed his long legs, he looked at Lucia more closely than he had before.

Any moment now...she thought.

And a few seconds later it happened: he switched on a different part of his brain and it processed her name and came up with all the facts it had been ignoring.

His grey eyes suddenly cold, he said, 'We've met before...in court. You're the forger.'

Lucia said a silent goodbye to the gift from the gods. She ought to have known it couldn't work out. Life just wasn't like that.

'Yes,' she said quietly.

'What the hell are you doing in this house?' He didn't raise his voice, but his eyes were like lasers.

'Lucia is here at my invitation,' said his mother. 'I knew she was being released this morning. I sent Jackson to fetch her. As you know, I was never happy about the court's decision, but now it's over and done with. She needs help getting back on her feet, and I need help with my travel plans.'

'Mother, you're out of your mind.'

Before Mrs Calderwood could reply, a telephone on the small table beside her chair began to ring.

'Excuse me,' she said to Lucia. Then, 'Hello? Mary...how nice to hear from you. Would you mind holding on for a minute? I'll be right back.' As she rose from her chair, she said to the others, 'I'll take this call in the study. Do help yourself to more coffee, Lucia.' A moment later she had stepped outside and vanished.

With the instinctive reflex of a man brought up in a family where old-fashioned courtesies were maintained,

Grey Calderwood had risen while his mother was leaving the room. Now, still on his feet, he scowled down at Lucia. 'It isn't a year since you were sentenced. What are you doing out of prison?'

'I've been allowed early-release.' She leaned forward to pick up the coffee pot. 'Would you like another cup, Mr Calderwood?'

He shook his head. 'Has my mother been in touch with you while you were in prison?'

'No, never. This morning, before I was released, the governor told me there was someone willing to help me rebuild my life. A car was waiting outside the prison gates. I met Mrs Calderwood when I got here.'

'My mother has a quixotic nature. Sometimes she allows it to overrule her common sense,' he said coldly. 'The governor would have done better to put you in touch with the various organisations that help released prisoners. While he's taking you to wherever you wish to go, you can use Jackson's mobile to call a Citizens' Advice Bureau. They'll put you in touch with the right people to help you.'

It took all Lucia's concentration to keep her hand steady as she refilled her cup. Before her arrest and imprisonment, she had been a self-confident person, a good mixer. They were characteristics, once effortless and taken for granted, that she would have to relearn. She was all right with someone friendly, like Mrs Calderwood, but the son, now that he had turned hostile, was harder for her to handle. He sapped her shaky *amour propre* merely by looking at her.

'I would like to accept the post your mother has offered me,' she told him.

'Out of the question,' he snapped. 'If my mother is determined to go on these trips, it's essential she has someone with her who has impeccable references and will be absolutely reliable. Not someone fresh out of prison for a serious offence.' His voice had the same cold ring she remembered from the court room.

'But not the kind of offence that makes me an unsafe person to be in charge of young children or elderly people.'

'That depends. In my judgment you are not a suitable companion for my mother.'

'Isn't that for her to decide?'

His mouth compressed in a hard line. The dark grey eyes flashed like steel blades.

'Perhaps a hand-out will persuade you to see reason.' He went to the chair where he had left his coat and took a cheque book from an inside pocket. As she watched he uncapped an expensive black fountain pen.

She watched him writing the cheque, wondering what he would consider a suitable pay-off. Although she had disliked the man from the moment he stepped into the witness box and looked across the court room as if, in his opinion, she was as despicable as a drug dealer or a child abuser, a part of her mind was forced to admire the articulation of his long strong fingers.

'There...that should cover your overheads until they find you a job.' He held out the cheque.

Lucia took it, curious to see what he was prepared to pay her. Her parents had not been well-off even when both were working, her father as a reporter on a provincial city's evening newspaper, her mother as a public librarian. There had never been a time when Lucia hadn't had to be careful with her own earnings. She couldn't imagine being able to scrawl a cheque with three noughts as casually as people dropped spare change in a charity worker's collecting tin.

The amount he had written in figures and numbers took her breath away. Particularly as there was no element of kindness involved. Clearly, he didn't want to help her. She felt he wouldn't have cared if her sentence had been ten times as long.

'But don't take it into your head that there might be more where that came from,' he said cuttingly. 'It's a one-off payment that will never be repeated. I'm making it on condition that you vanish from our lives and don't reappear...ever. In the circumstances, it's exceedingly generous of me to offer you any help. If you show up again, you'll regret it. I can make big trouble for you—and will. You had better believe that.'

'Oh, I do. You already have,' she said dryly, folding the cheque in two and then in four.

'You brought that on yourself, though I dare say you'll never admit it. You'd rather believe the sob story cooked up by your lawyer.'

There was no point in arguing with him. He was the type of man who, privileged from birth, could never understand the actions that had led to her arrest.

Mrs Calderwood rejoined them. 'I'm sorry I had to leave you.'

'Ms Graham has changed her mind about the job you offered her,' said Grey. 'She realises it wouldn't suit her.'

His mother was not a fool. She obviously knew that her son liked to have his own way.

Looking disappointed, she said, 'Did Grey make up your mind, or is that your own decision?'

Acting on instinct, Lucia had palmed the cheque before Mrs Calderwood saw it. Knowing that Grey would make a dangerous enemy but still impelled to defy him, she said, 'Mr Calderwood would like it to be my decision, but it's not. If you're really sure I will suit you, I'd be happy to work for you.'

'That's splendid,' said Rosemary Calderwood, ignoring her son's silent but visible fury. 'Now I'm sure you must be longing for a bath and a change of clothes. I've already sorted out some things left here by my daughters that you can wear till we have time to go shopping.'

'I thought you might need some more coffee,' said the grey-haired woman, coming back.

'This is Mrs Bradley, my housekeeper,' said Rosemary. 'Miss Graham is joining us, Braddy. Would you show her where she can bath and change before lunch?'

'One moment,' Grey said sharply. 'Mother, I don't often interfere in your arrangements, but this time I must. I cannot allow you to employ this young woman.'

He looked so stern and fierce that Lucia half expected his mother to yield to the force of his authority. She had already admitted to letting her late husband quash her youthful ambitions. It seemed unlikely she would resist her son if he chose to put his foot down.

But it seemed that Rosemary's will had strengthened not weakened with age. She said pleasantly, 'I appreciate your concern for my welfare, my dear, but please don't use that dictatorial tone to me. Your father laid down the law for fifty years. From now on I shall do as I think best.' With a sweeping gesture of her hand she sent Mrs Bradley and Lucia on their way, before saying to her son, 'You are staying to lunch, I hope, darling? I'm the cook today. We're having lamb cutlets with tapenade.'

It was a long time since Lucia had had a leisurely wallow in a bath of warm scented water. Even then her bath accessories had not been of the quality provided for her use in this luxurious bathroom. As well as a pale blue face cloth to match the thick fluffy towels, there was a huge sponge and a two-handled strap with a strip of loofah on one side and towelling on the other. On a recessed tiled shelf in the wall behind the bath there were bottles and tubes of foams, gels and bath oils. There was nothing anyone could want in the way of toiletries that hadn't been provided, including the pretty shower cap still hanging on its peg and the white terry robe draped over a heated towel rail at one end of the bath-cum-shower alcove as an alternative to the towels.

Seeing a hair dryer on the counter surrounding the handbasin, she had asked Mrs Bradley if there would be time to wash her hair. The housekeeper had said yes, plenty of time. Lunch would be served at one, leaving an hour to spare.

The bath, designed to accommodate a tall male house guest, was long enough for Lucia to slide down and immerse her hair. As she was doing this, there was a peremptory knock on the unlocked door and Grey Calderwood stalked in.

CHAPTER TWO

FOR some seconds she was too startled to react. Then, as a couple of strides brought him to where a bath mat protected the pale fitted carpet, she sat up in a hurry, making the water slosh dangerously close to the rim while she grabbed the sponge in an effort to cover her breasts.

'How dare you burst in here?' she flared at him.

'How dare you take my cheque and then break the deal?' he retorted, his cold eyes taking in her nakedness.

There had been times in prison when she had hated the lack of privacy and felt frighteningly vulnerable to unwelcome advances. This was different, but equally disturbing. She knew there was no possibility he would snatch the sponge or touch her. He might be a pig, but he wasn't that kind of pig. At least she didn't think he was. Nevertheless she felt furious at being caught with dripping hair and a lot of bare flesh on view.

'You'll find the cheque on the dressing table. I never had any intention of cashing it. Take it and get out,' she snapped at him.

'Not until I've made some things clear to you. My mother refuses to listen to reason. But don't congratulate yourself on landing a cushy number here. If you step out of line by so much as a centimetre, I'll make you regret you were born. You got off lightly last time. You won't again. I'll make sure of that.'

Lucia was tempted to respond with a mouthful of the hair-raising invective she had learned while she was

17

'banged up', as habitual law-breakers called being behind bars. But even after spending months among women whose language, at the beginning, had often made her flinch inwardly, she still couldn't quite bring herself to use their vocabulary to vent her hostility towards him. Anyway swearing at him would only prove his point: that she wasn't fit to associate with a sheltered woman like his mother.

Swallowing her resentment of his unforgiving attitude, she said, 'I'm very grateful to your mother for extending a helping hand to me. I shan't abuse her trust.'

'See that you don't.' He walked out.

He and Mrs Calderwood were in the drawing room, chatting as if nothing untoward had happened, when Lucia joined them. From the clothes put out for her to wear, she had chosen a plain white shirt and a pair of pale khaki chinos.

As she entered, Grey rose. It was, she knew, an automatic reflex ingrained from boyhood. Actually he felt none of the chivalrous respect implied by the now-rare courtesy of standing up for her.

'What would you like to drink, Lucia?' Mrs Calderwood asked. 'Grey is having a gin and tonic and my pre-lunch tipple is always Campari and soda—unless I'm alone. I never drink on my own.'

'May I have a soft drink, please?' After months of abstinence, Lucia didn't want to risk her first taste of alcohol going to her head.

'Of course. Orange juice or peach juice?'

'Orange juice, please.'

Grey moved to an antique cupboard, the upper half containing glasses and bottles, the lower concealing a small fridge. He brought her a crystal goblet with ice cubes floating in the fruit juice. Rather than handing it to her, he placed it on the end table of the sofa which his mother had indicated her guest should share with her.

'Thank you.' Lucia wondered if he felt that physical contact with her, even of the most fleeting kind, might contaminate him. He had probably never had to socialise with an ex-prisoner before.

She had always known there would be people who would consider her unfit to mix in polite society. That was inevitable. She just hadn't expected to encounter that attitude on her first day outside.

'What were the meals like in prison?' Rosemary Calderwood asked. 'Like boarding school food, I imagine...lots of stodge and over-cooked vegetables.'

Lucia nodded. 'Chips with everything and not enough salad. But then prison isn't supposed to be like a pleasure cruise.'

'No, but they should feed people properly. You look as if you're several pounds under your proper weight. We'll soon put that right. Both Braddy and I are excellent cooks and we have a big kitchen garden so our vegetables haven't been grown under plastic and spent days being transported to a supermarket. I'm a bit of a health freak. My children tease me about it, but I do most strongly believe we are what we eat.'

Obviously aware of the antagonism between her son and her protégée, Rosemary kept a conversation going with the skill of an accomplished hostess. From time to time she forced her son to take part with a question or comment that he was obliged to respond to. Lucia was glad to pick up the cues she gave her. If it hadn't been for Grey's presence, she would have been in heaven.

The elegant room, with its paintings, antiques, oriental rugs and bowls of freshly-cut flowers from the garden outside was balm to her beauty-starved senses.

Presently they moved to the dining room where three places had been laid at the end of a long polished table.

Grey drew out the chair at the end for his mother. Lucia seated herself. Then Mrs Bradley came in with the first course, a dish of grilled aubergines garnished with chopped herbs and crumbled feta cheese.

'Will you have some wine?' Grey asked, after pouring a pale golden liquid into his mother's glass.

Lucia decided one glass would be OK. 'Yes, please.'

He moved round the table, standing close to her chair, making her strangely conscious of his nearness, his masculinity. Was it only because she was used to an almost exclusively female environment? The prison doctor and the chaplain were the only men she had seen during her time inside.

Compared with the fare provided since her arrest, the aubergines were almost unbearably delicious. Then came the cutlets, decorated with strips of red pepper and served with a bulghur wheat salad containing diced cucumber, chopped spring onions, toasted pine nuts and fresh mint. The tapenade mentioned earlier turned out to be the black olive paste smeared on the cutlets.

While they were eating, Grey suddenly asked her, 'Are you wearing a PID?'

Before Lucia, startled by this abrupt return to hostilities, could answer him, his mother said, 'What is a PID?'

'Ms Graham will explain,' said Grey, eyeing her with undisguised dislike.

'PID stands for Personal Identification Device,' Lucia said evenly. 'It's about the size of a diver's watch, but it can be attached to the ankle as well as the wrist. It sends a signal to a radio receiver called a Home Monitoring Unit. If the monitor can't detect the signal, it sends a message to the Monitoring Centre where records are kept of offenders and their curfew orders. It's a way of keeping a check on people who, like me, have been released early.'

She had been speaking to Mrs Calderwood, but now looked directly at her son. 'But I'm not wearing one, Mr Calderwood. They must have thought it wasn't necessary. I haven't been given any curfew instructions.'

'Possibly not, but I think you will find that you're not completely at liberty,' he said sternly. 'It's unlikely the conditions of your release will permit you to leave the country. If you can't go abroad, you're of little use to my mother.'

This was an aspect of the situation that Lucia hadn't considered. She had a sinking feeling he might be right.

'That point was raised by Miss Harris when we discussed Lucia's case,' said Mrs Calderwood. 'Luckily I have a friend at court, as they say. Or, rather more usefully in this instance, at the Home Office. He kindly pulled some strings for me. In view of the fact that I was a magistrate for twenty years, it was decided I was a suitable person to supervise Lucia's life until she is free to go where she pleases. As long as she is with me, there are no restrictions on her movements.'

This announcement made Grey look even more forbidding. Clearly, he had thought he was playing a trump card and was furious to find himself trumped.

Lucia wondered if he also had friends in high places whose influence he could bring to bear. He struck her as a man who, once he had put his mind to something, would not easily be defeated. There was obstinacy, even ruthlessness, in the jut of his jaw.

The meal ended with a rhubarb compote served with whipped cream.

Forgetting for a moment the constraint imposed by the man on the other side of the table, Lucia said to her hostess, 'I shall remember this lunch all my life. It was a lovely meal by any standards, but for me...' She made an expressive gesture.

'Good: I'm glad you enjoyed it. As it's such a warm day, let's have coffee on the terrace, shall we? Then I'll take you round the garden. Since all the children left home, gardening has been my principal occupation,' Rosemary told her. 'But now I'm beginning to find that I can't kneel and bend as comfortably as I used to. So I'm turning more and more to painting. The wheel is turning full circle.'

'After coffee I must be off. I shouldn't really have skived off,' said Grey.

Just as Lucia was thinking that the slang expression for evading one's responsibilities or duties sounded odd coming from him, he glanced at her and she knew he was thinking, But it's fortunate that I did or I wouldn't have known about you.

'You work too hard,' said his mother. 'Don't become like your father...a workaholic. There is more to life than doing business.'

Lucia wasn't sure what Grey did for his living. It must be something highly profitable if he could afford to spend six-figure sums of money on paintings. At the time of the trial, the tabloids had described him as a 'tycoon and art connoisseur' always giving his age, thirty-six, after his name.

As almost the only people who had made vast fortunes at his age were the Internet billionaires, and somehow he didn't look like Britain's answer to Bill Gates, it seemed likely he had inherited the fruits of his father's workaholicism.

The opulence of his parents' house, and the fact that his mother had spent her life being a homemaker, indicated that Calderwood Senior had been a man of substantial means.

Grey made no comment on his mother's admonition. Perhaps it was one he had heard many times before and didn't take seriously. He gave the impression of being a man who would always do what he thought best, regardless of advice.

He was one of those people—Lucia had met a few others—who came over as being propelled by a strong driving force. But what form his took and where it was driving him, she didn't yet know. Most likely it was money or power, or both. Those seemed to be the two most common motivations among the male sex. She preferred creative people…artists, musicians, poets. Grey probably looked at paintings as investments rather than food for the spirit.

The stone-flagged terrace on the south side of the house was furnished with comfortable cane chairs and loungers. As she sipped her coffee, Lucia would have liked to lie back and snooze.

It had been a taxing day: being released, then being whisked away on a magical mystery tour, then crossing swords with Grey had made it stressful as well as memorable. She had hardly slept last night. Now she was finding it hard to keep her eyes open…

*   *   *

Driving back to London, Grey blamed himself for not foreseeing and averting his mother's ill-conceived plan to help the Graham girl find her feet.

His part in bringing the fraudsters to justice had worried her. He loved his mother and his sisters, but they were all the same; sentimental liberal do-gooders who could find excuses for everything except cruelty to animals and children and crimes against humanity. And even in those cases they were inclined to look for reasons why the perpetrators had done what they'd done.

Grey didn't belong to the pity-the-victims-of-society brigade. He didn't regard himself a hard man, but he was a realist. At the time of the trial he had felt no regret for being instrumental in exposing a scam, helping to stop it and seeing the culprits suitably punished.

Now, having met Lucia, he was a good deal less comfortable with the thought of what she had been through.

He remembered how she had looked in the bath and how, to increase his annoyance, he had found himself aroused by the sight of her breasts. At first, as she lay submerged, they had floated like two pale islands with rose-coloured crests. Then, as she sat up in a hurry, they had changed shape and, for a fleeting moment before she concealed them with her forearms and the sponge, formed two exquisite half-spheres that had instantly triggered a strong reaction in his groin.

Perversely, the fact that her body excited him had made him snarl at her even more fiercely than he had intended. Had her alluring looks made her the target for advances from the tough, amoral, sexually frustrated women who were bound to be found among any prison's inmates and possibly among those who ran such places?

The fact that Lucia was what his mother's peer group called 'a lady' would have made her even more of a target for the kind of prisoner or warder who resented people whose lives had been more privileged than theirs.

He had an unpleasant vision of Lucia being locked up in a cell with hardened and unscrupulous criminals from whom she would have no escape. The picture revolted and enraged him to the extent that, several minutes later, he realised he had unconsciously increased his pressure on the throttle to the extent that the car was streaking down the overtaking lane at well beyond the motorway limit.

Reducing speed, he switched his mind to matters that had nothing to do with the girl who, when last seen, had fallen into a deep sleep.

'She's exhausted, poor child. Let's leave her and go for a stroll,' his mother had whispered.

Later, saying goodbye to him, she had said, 'You aren't cross with me for putting you down before lunch, are you? Your father would have been furious, but I don't think your ego is quite as large or as sensitive as his was, thank goodness. Although I loved him, I didn't always like him, you know. We were never the friends and equals that married people should be...that I hope you and your wife, when you find her, will be.'

The truth, though he hadn't admitted it, was that he had been angry when, in front of the two other women, she had told him off for being dictatorial. But he could never be angry with her for long. Many times, when he was feeling his oats and before he had learnt how to handle his domineering father, she had averted clashes between them. He knew she had paid a high price for loving a man who, though he claimed to worship her, had expected her to conform to his idea of the perfect wife and never allowed her the freedom to adapt that role to her own needs.

Grey knew she was longing for him to emulate his sisters by marrying and starting a family. He didn't think that was going to happen. He had enjoyed a number of relationships with women, but he had never met one who tempted him to give up his freedom. He didn't think he ever would.

When Lucia woke up she found herself alone with Rosemary who was working on a piece of needlepoint.

'I'm sorry. How long have I been asleep?'

'Just over an hour. No need to apologise. You needed it. Grey has gone back to London. He lives by the river which is as nice as living in a big city can ever be. I can stand it for forty-eight hours, but after that claustrophobia sets in. I need to get back to the country. I'll tell Braddy you're awake. We'll have some tea and then I'll take you on a tour.'

At seven they had a light lap supper while watching the news on TV. Then there was a gardening programme Rosemary wanted to watch, followed by a repeat of a popular comedy show.

When that was over, she said, 'If I were you I should have an early night, or at least read in bed. You'll find a selection of books that I thought might interest you on your bedside table.'

As they both rose, Lucia said, 'I don't know how to thank you for being willing to give me this chance. I'll do my best to make sure you never regret it.'

'I'm quite sure I shan't,' Rosemary said kindly. 'Goodnight, Lucia. I hope you sleep well. Tomorrow we'll plan our first expedition together.'

To Lucia's astonishment, Grey's mother placed her

hands on her shoulders and kissed her lightly on both
cheeks.

During her time in prison she had found she could
bear the bullying of some of the screws, as the prisoners
called the prison officers, and the hostile behaviour of
some of her fellow inmates. It was always the unexpected kindnesses that had weakened her self-control.

Now the affectionate gesture brought a lump to her
throat and made her eyes fill with tears. But it wasn't
until she was alone in her room that she flung herself
into an armchair and indulged in the luxury of weeping.

Later, after washing her face, brushing her hair and
teeth, and putting on the hand-smocked white voile
nightgown spread across the turned-down bed, she
opened the curtains and turned out the lights.

Tonight she didn't feel like reading. She just wanted
to lie in the comfortable bed and watch the moon
through an unbarred window and try to accustom herself to this miraculous change in her fortunes.

Whether she could ever win Grey's good opinion
seemed doubtful. In his view, and that of many other
people, she would probably carry the stigma of her
crime for the rest of her life. It was a lowering prospect:
never, in some people's estimation, to be re-admitted to
the ranks of the honest and honourable.

Then, as her lips began to quiver and she felt another
bout of crying coming on, she told herself not to be a
wimp. What did it matter if Grey continued to despise
her? Rich and arrogant, what did he know about ordi-
nary people's lives and the pressures they had to bear?

Clearly he wasn't accustomed to anyone defying him.
Most likely he would blame Lucia for his mother's re-
fusal to accept his embargo on her plan. It was also
likely he would look for ways to enforce his will.

If he did, she would resist him, as she had this morning when he had tried to buy her off. From what she had seen of 'Mr Grey' as the housekeeper called him, Lucia felt it might do him a great deal of good to have someone around who would refuse to kowtow to him.

CHAPTER THREE

LUCIA was woken by birdsong.

She lay listening to what she realised must be the dawn chorus as heard in the depths of the country. Compared with the twitterings at first light of suburban and city birds, it was like someone whose only experience of choral music had been a small school choir hearing, for the first time, the chorus of a grand opera company. After a while it died down and she drifted back to sleep until something else woke her. This time the room was full of sunlight and Mrs Bradley was bringing in a breakfast tray.

'Mrs Calderwood thinks you should take it easy for a few days,' said the housekeeper, after they had exchanged good mornings. 'She'll be up to see you presently. You can eat eggs, I hope?'

'I can eat anything,' Lucia assured her.

After the housekeeper had gone, she nipped out of bed to brush her teeth before drinking some of the chilled orange juice. Under the silver-plated dome with a handle on the top was a perfectly poached egg, with the deep orange yolk only produced by hens who could peck where they pleased, on a thick slice of toasted brown bread. Several more slices of toast were swathed in a thick napkin inside a basket, next to a little dish filled with curls of butter and a glass pot of thick-cut marmalade that, like the bread, looked home-made.

After months of enduring the horrible breakfasts in prison, Lucia relished every mouthful. She was pouring the last of the tea into her cup when there was a tap on the door and Rosemary appeared.

'Good morning. What sort of night did you have?'

'Wonderful, thank you.'

'Good. I'm told that coming out of prison is like being discharged from hospital after a major operation. It's best to take things rather slowly…re-adapt at a leisurely pace. I thought this morning we'd take the dogs for a walk. They belong to my eldest daughter Julia and her husband. They're visiting a game reserve in Africa. Leaving the dogs with me is preferable to boarding them in kennels.'

Later, while they were walking an elderly golden retriever and two energetic Jack Russells, she said, 'Perhaps you've wondered why I didn't visit you in prison to introduce myself before you came here?'

'I hadn't thought about it,' said Lucia.

'I felt it might be an intrusion on the short time you were allowed to see people you knew,' Rosemary explained. 'Also I felt it would be difficult to make friends in those circumstances.'

'It would have been,' Lucia agreed.

She did not reveal that she had had no visitors. Some of the people who might have come to see her lived too far away. After giving up her last job to take care of her father during his long illness, she had lost touch with former colleagues. In their twenties, most people had too much going on in their own lives to bother with colleagues who had either been 'let go' or had dropped out for other reasons. Anyway, from what she had seen, visits from family members and friends could be more upsetting than pleasurable.

But she didn't want to think about what she had

learned in prison. She wanted to put it behind her and get to grips with the future.

'These painting trips you mentioned yesterday... where are you thinking of going?' she asked.

'I thought we might start with the Channel Islands before going further afield. Years ago, when the girls were small, we shared a house on Sark with some friends who also had young children. We took it for a month. Our husbands came over to join us at the weekends. Other years we went to France. Do you speak French, Lucia?'

'Not very much, I'm afraid.'

'Never mind. It's not important. I'm not a linguist myself, nor was my husband. I don't know where Grey gets his gift of tongues from.'

'Does he need them for his work?'

'Not specifically, but languages are always an asset. He does travel a lot, both for business and pleasure.'

In his spacious office on the top floor of a riverside tower block in London, Grey was pacing the thick carpet and thinking about the girl who, forty-eight hours ago, had still been locked up, and today was being cosseted by his mother, an expert at pampering anyone whom she considered needed it.

There were other things that he ought to be giving his mind and, normally, he kept his life neatly compartmentalised, focussing his whole attention on the compartment he was in. Right now that was the property business started by his grandfather, developed and expanded by his father, and now directed by himself.

But instead of being able to concentrate on matters pertaining to a major expansion, he was fidgeted by a strong hunch that, unless he found a way to get rid of her, that girl was going to cause trouble.

After pressing the bell for his personal assistant, he took another turn around the room.

When, notepad in hand, she appeared in the doorway, he said, 'Bring me the file on that court case I was involved in, would you, Alice? And I want to speak to my sister Jenny, if you can get her.'

Alice nodded and withdrew. A few moments later she reappeared with a black ring-binder and placed it on his desk.

He was leafing through the collection of press clippings, each one in a plastic pocket labelled with the date and source, when one of his telephones rang. He picked it up. 'Yes?'

'I have Mrs Wentworth on the line, Mr Calderwood.'

'Put her on, please. Hello, Jenny. How are you?' He listened to her reply, then said, 'Are you free this weekend? Splendid. Then call Mum and invite yourself to lunch on Sunday, will you? I'd like your opinion on her latest lame duck.'

The news that Rosemary's youngest daughter was coming to lunch made Lucia a little nervous, but she knew that meeting people was something she must get used to.

It was when Mrs Calderwood added, 'And Grey is coming too,' that her nervousness moved up a gear, though she hoped her face didn't show it.

'Does he visit you often?' she asked.

'As often as he can…but he's very busy,' his mother replied. 'Jenny's husband, Tom, is more laid-back than Grey. He's an architect in a partnership. That isn't always plain sailing, but it's nothing like as onerous as the burden on Grey. In these tough, competitive times, having to make decisions that affect a very large workforce is a massive responsibility. It's what brought on my husband's health problems. But Grey keeps himself fit. Robert used to play golf, but I don't think that was as good for him as the swimming and fencing and workouts that Grey goes in for.'

'What is his business?' Lucia asked.

'His grandfather was a builder. He never made very much money from the business but he put what money he had into buying land on the outskirts of towns. You may not have heard of a Hollywood film star and comedian called Bob Hope, but he was very famous in his day. He was my father-in-law's favourite star, and somewhere he had read that Bob Hope put most of his earnings from movies into buying up land on the outskirts of American towns. So my father-in-law did the same thing. He didn't benefit from it but Robert, my husband, did. It enabled him to expand the business in all sorts of directions. By the time Grey left university, it was one of the largest private companies in the country.'

Lucia had already learned that the Calderwoods had almost despaired of having a son. As well as having three daughters, Rosemary had had two miscarriages. Then, aged thirty-four, she had conceived again. She had had to spend most of her sixth pregnancy in bed but, at the end of it, had produced the longed-for male child.

With doting parents and three older sisters, Grey must have been spoiled rotten from birth, was Lucia's conclusion.

She wondered why he wasn't married. The possibility that he might not be heterosexual had occurred to her but been dismissed. In her working life, as a commercial artist, she had met a lot of gay men. Sometimes it was difficult, on slight acquaintance, to tell their orientation. But none gave off the kind of vibes that Grey did. She was certain all his sexual relationships were with women, and that they had been and would always be the most gorgeous chicks available. With his looks and position and money, why would he ever settle for anything less than a combination of glamour and intelligence?

On Sunday morning Rosemary went to church in the nearby village. She asked if Lucia would like to go with her but did not appear to mind when she declined. Although it was unlikely that anyone attending morning service in the small parish church would recognise her from newspaper pictures published months ago, Lucia wasn't ready to face the world yet. The family lunch party was enough of an ordeal for one day.

Since her arrival she had washed and ironed the jeans, shirt and sweater she had worn to come here. Today she was wearing her own things in preference to those that Rosemary kindly lent her. Her other clothes, like the rest of her possessions, were in storage. Not that she had a lot of stuff. Only clothes and books and her painting things.

Mrs Calderwood had not returned from church and Lucia was in the dining room, making herself useful by laying the table according to Mrs Bradley's directions, when she saw a car in the drive. As it drew up in front of the house, she recognised it as a Jaguar, the make her father would have liked to own had he had enough money. The driver was Grey.

He got out but instead of turning towards the house, he stood facing the garden, stretching his arms and then flexing his broad shoulders. Today he was casually dressed in chinos and a blue shirt with the sleeves folded to mid-forearm.

Before he could turn and catch her watching him, she withdrew to the inner end of the room where he wouldn't see her.

Instead of heading for the front door, he went round the side of the house and a short time later she heard him speaking to the housekeeper on the other side of the door that led to the kitchen. It was a thick door and she couldn't hear their conversation, only the two voices, one deeper and more resonant than the other.

Then the connecting door opened and he walked into the dining room, making her spine prickle with apprehension.

Mustering her self-possession, she said politely, 'Good morning.'

'Good morning. When you've finished in here, I'd like to talk to you. Braddy's making me some coffee. I'll be on the terrace.'

Taking her compliance for granted, he withdrew.

Wondering what she was going to hear, Lucia completed her task. She had chosen and arranged the flowers in containers from a large selection on the shelves of what had once been a scullery.

'Small, low arrangements please, Lucia,' Mrs Calderwood had said, before leaving for church. 'We want to be able to see each other.'

From a variety of possibilities, Lucia had chosen hem-stitched linen place mats in a colour to tone with the flowers. Beneath them were heat-proof pads and, on three sides, mellow Georgian silver knives, forks and spoons. The side plates were antique Spode bone china, the large folded napkins linen in a colour to tone with the mats. The fine sheen of the table's surface reflected everything on it in a way that made her long to paint it.

Grey was standing up, drinking coffee from a yellow mug, when she joined him.

'Have you had coffee?' he asked.

'Yes, thank you…earlier.'

He gestured for her to sit down then seated himself in a chair at right angles to hers.

'Where would you have gone if my mother hadn't intervened? Presumably they don't release you without checking that you have somewhere to go or money for food and lodging?'

'I was planning to collect one of my suitcases and find a bed-and-breakfast place. The flat I was living in before was only rented.'

'Where is your suitcase?'

'There are two, but I would only have needed the one with my clothes and hair dryer and so on. I packed them and put them in storage while I was out on bail, between being arrested and sentenced. My lawyer expected a suspended sentence but I thought it was best to prepare for the worst.'

'What does "in storage" mean?'

'They're in a furniture repository near where I used to live.'

He raised a dark eyebrow. 'Why not with friends or relations?'

'I don't have any close relations. Both my parents were only children. Two cases aren't the sort of thing you dump on people unless they have a lot more room than any of the people I knew did. Your living quarters are probably much more spacious than most people's, but would you want to be encumbered by someone else's suitcases?'

He thought about that for a moment. 'It would depend on the strength of the friendship.'

'My two closest friends weren't around. One of them works in New York and the other is married to an Italian. They live in Milan.'

'So you're on your own?'

'Yes, but that's no big deal. Most people are on their own these days, Mr Calderwood. Large, close families like yours aren't the norm any more. It's mostly a "singles" world now.'

'I know and I wish it weren't,' he said frowning. 'The way things are going isn't good for anyone. It's not good for society as a whole and it plays hell with children's lives. But it's not my sex that's to blame for the breakdown of family life. That's down to your sex. It may still be a man's world—just—but the direction it's taking is a consequence of women's initiatives.'

'What do you mean?'

Before he could answer, the sound of the front bell could be heard through the open door that led from the terrace to the hall.

'That'll be my sister and her husband.' He rose to go and let them in.

Wondering if Rosemary had told them her history, Lucia picked up his empty mug and took it to the kitchen. She would have liked to know what Grey would have replied if they hadn't been interrupted, but it was unlikely he would resume the topic in the presence of the others and it wasn't likely she would be alone with him again today.

She had rinsed out the mug and was drying it when

Mrs Calderwood came through the dining room door. 'I'm back. How are things going, Braddy?'

'Everything's under control.'

'Good: I'll get you your drink, introduce Lucia, and come back and make my special dressing for the starter.' Beckoning Lucia to accompany her, Rosemary headed for the door leading to the rear of the hall.

As she had put on a dress to go to church, Lucia had worried that her jeans might be too informal for today's lunch. To her relief, her benefactor's daughter was also wearing jeans, though her top was recognisably one of a famous designer's expensively beautiful knits and Lucia's was a schoolboy-sized shirt she had found on the men's rail in a charity shop.

Before Rosemary could introduce them, her daughter jumped up, put out her hand and said, 'Hi, I'm Jenny…and you're Mum's unlikely-looking jailbird. Nice to meet you. This is my husband Tom.'

A thickset man with a receding hairline and kind blue eyes offered his hand. 'Hello, Lucia. I'm an architect…married to a woman who prides herself on her outspokenness which is why some people cross the road when they see us coming. The first time we met she told me I stank of garlic.'

'But I liked him so much that, despite the garlic, *I* kissed *him* goodnight…and he came back for more and here we are twenty years later,' said Jenny, laughing. 'What are you going to drink, Lucia? White wine?'— with a flourish of her own glass.

'Yes, please.'

Grey was in the act of handing a Campari and soda to his mother. He glanced at Lucia. 'Jenny likes her wine sweet. Would you rather have something dryer?'

At first she had been taken aback by Jenny's immediate reference to her imprisonment. Now she was grateful to her for bringing it into the open so quickly, and to Tom for picking up what some would regard as his wife's indiscretion and capping it in an amusing way. It was immediately obvious that they were very happy together.

'What Jenny is drinking will be fine.' Smiling at his sister, she said, 'Drinking anything alcoholic is a major treat for me. There was some illicit alcohol available in prison—at a price—but I wasn't desperate enough to risk it.'

'Was there anyone like yourself in there? Anyone you could be friendly with?'

'In prison, you're grateful if anyone will be friendly with you,' Lucia said quietly. But she knew it was next to impossible to make people who had never been there understand how it was 'inside'.

Jenny started to ask something else but was stopped by her brother saying, 'Don't start grilling her, Jen.' Putting a glass of wine into Lucia's hand, he said, 'My sister was once a journalist...more precisely a junior reporter on a small town weekly. It was going to lead to a glittering career in London, but she met Tom and changed her mind.'

'And have never regretted it,' said Jenny. 'I enjoyed my three years on the Gazette, but I like being my own boss better. Now that the children are launched, I may try a spot of freelancing.'

'Did you read the article in yesterday's paper...?' Tom took charge of the conversation and steered it in a more general direction.

diana referred it to her for comment. Now she was
grateful to her for bringing it into the open so quickly
and to Tom for picking up what some would regard as
this wretched woman's . . . . in as unfussy a
way it was . . . . obvious that they were very

CHAPTER FOUR

HALF an hour later, starting to eat his lunch, Grey wondered why, when he had engineered his sister's presence
here in order for her to exercise her canny judgment of
character on the interloper in their midst, he had chosen
to intervene when she started questioning Lucia.

Something in Lucia's face as she answered Jenny's
first question had stirred a curious sense of compunction
in him. Logically it was she who should be feeling that
reaction.

He looked up from the grilled courgettes dressed with
a special apple and caper mixture of his mother's and
glanced across the table. Today his mother was at the
head of it, with Tom and himself on either side of her
and Lucia on the left of his brother-in-law. They seemed
to be getting on well while Jenny talked across him to
their mother.

He watched Lucia laughing at something Tom had
said to her. With him, she seemed wholly relaxed. With
himself she was tense and guarded. As she bloody well
should be, he thought, remembering that she had cost
him a very large sum of money, not to mention considerable loss of face. He could live with that aspect of the
affair rather better than the fine art auctioneers from
whom he had bought the fake painting they had au-
thenticated as a genuine pencil and watercolour drawing
by Joseph Edward Southall.

Their reputation was in shreds, his own only dented.
That the prime mover of the scam was the guy who was

still in prison, and who would remain there for several years, was beside the point. Without Lucia's skill he could not have carried out the operation.

Grey wondered if their relationship had gone beyond business dealings. Later on he would ask her. Or perhaps ask Jenny to find out. With his sister's gift for winning people's confidence, she was more likely to elicit the truth than he was.

Lucia did not give the impression of being a woman of considerable sexual experience. There was nothing bold or even confident about her. Her reaction to his invasion of the bathroom the other day had been almost virginal. But she could be and probably was putting on an act. Like a cat, she had fallen on her feet and was far too astute to muff this unexpected opportunity to enjoy the good life at someone else's expense.

On the other side of the table, Lucia was aware of being under surveillance. It made it difficult for her to give Tom her full attention. He was telling her about a Scottish architect who had set up his practice in 1848 and, designing houses for newly-rich Glasgow merchants and factory owners, had evolved a style that was now regarded as the finest neo-classical urban design anywhere.

'The tragedy is that until quite recently Thomson's buildings were being demolished,' Tom told her. 'One of his best buildings, with black marble fireplaces and fine ceiling decorations, was sledge-hammered into rubble.'

'What a shame.' Lucia was sincere in deploring the destruction, but try as she might she could not switch off her awareness of the cold gaze she knew was focussed on her.

If Grey hadn't been present she could have enjoyed herself. The courgettes and their sauce were delicious. Tom and his wife seemed willing to take it on trust that she had paid for her misdemeanours and would not repeat them.

Only Grey seemed determined to distrust her. Was that only because he was the only person here who had been directly affected by the fraud in which she had conspired, if not knowingly and directly then at least by refusing to listen to the questions asked by her conscience?

Or did Grey have other reasons for being wary, not just of her but of the whole female sex? The remark he had made before his sister's arrival—about the direction the world was taking being a consequence of women's initiatives—hinted at some kind of hang-up connected with feminist issues.

Lucia belonged to the post-feminist generation. She knew Grey was thirty-six, twelve years older than herself, because his mother, now seventy, had told her he was born when she was thirty-four. Probably, when he was twenty, more vulnerable than he was now, he would have encountered some feminist extremists and attitudes far more hostile than those that were prevalent now.

After lunch they all went for a walk, setting out in a group but gradually separating into a threesome and a twosome, the latter being herself and Jenny bringing up the rear while the two men walked on either side of Rosemary.

'Now I *can* grill you about the prison,' said Jenny, with a sideways grin. 'I must admit I'm madly curious...who wouldn't be? Do you mind if I ask you questions? If you really don't want to talk about it, I'll shut up.'

'I don't mind—but first I'd like to ask you something,' said Lucia.

'Fair enough…go ahead.'

'How do you feel about my being your mother's painting companion on these trips that she's planning? I know Grey isn't happy with the arrangement. Do you share his reservations?'

As she spoke she looked at the three people strolling ahead of them along the grassy ride through an area of private woodland whose owner had given Mrs Calderwood permission to walk there.

She was a tallish woman, about five-eight to Lucia's five-six. Tom was probably five-ten and Grey topped him by two or three inches. Had she known nothing about him, from the way he carried himself she might have surmised that he was a professional soldier. He looked like an off-duty army colonel rather than a fat-cat businessman.

At that moment he broke his stride to put his foot on a felled tree at the side of the ride and retie the lace of his shoe. As the movement pulled the seat of his chinos tight across his backside and outlined the muscular thigh of the leg he had raised, she felt a stirring inside her that she recognised as desire.

It annoyed her that the physical appeal of a man who didn't like her, and who she had no reason to like, could affect her so strongly. It was not as if she had had an active sex life before being imprisoned and was impatient to resume it. The months of nursing her father had cut her off from most social contacts. Even before that, when she was working at the agency, she had never been comfortable with the casual relationships that some of her colleagues and contacts regarded as normal.

To Lucia, sex was meaningless unless it was accompanied, at the very least, by some warmth and tenderness. Which made it all the more annoying that a man who didn't like her and whom she had no reason to like could arouse these disturbing feelings in her.

'There's a lot of my father in Grey,' said Jenny, after giving Lucia's question some thought. 'I loved Dad, although it has to be said that he was a prime example of a male supremacist. But then most of his generation were. I'm certain that, once he was married, he was totally faithful to Mum. But it wouldn't have occurred to him that she needed something more than to be his adoring slave. He would have given his life for her...but he didn't want her to have any life of her own that wasn't centred around him. Grey has inherited that protective instinct—at least with women related to him,' she added, in a dry tone. 'I have more confidence in Mum's ability to look out for herself. *Do* you have any ulterior motives?' she added bluntly.

'How could I have? I didn't know I was coming here until I arrived. I still feel I'm going to wake up and find I've been dreaming. After all, she has more reason than most to dislike me. Her son was one of the people who got hurt.'

'Only in his pocket,' said Jenny. 'My impression, from reading the evidence, is that you were a victim yourself. The guy who's still in clink...were you and he an item?'

Lucia remembered the day Alec had made a pass at her. Knowing that he was only trying it on because every halfway presentable woman was a challenge to him, she had forced herself to rebuff him. But she hadn't wanted to. In a flashy way, he was attractive, and she was lonely and hungry for the love that was a long time coming.

'No,' she said. 'It was strictly a business relationship.'

'And none of your pre-prison boyfriends was close enough to be waiting outside the gates when they let you out?'

'No.'

'I could be wrong, but I'm inclined to take you at your face value,' said Jenny. 'You look to me like a person I'd trust to keep an eye on my luggage while I went to the loo on a train. Not, come to think of it, that that's taking a huge risk,' she added, smiling. 'At least not on a train in this country. According to our back-packing children, there are countries where you need to hang onto your stuff every single second or someone will swipe it from under your very nose.'

She began to tell Lucia some of her children's adventures.

At the end of the ride there was another five-barred gate to climb. Grey swung himself over it in one easy moment and stood ready to put out a steadying hand while his mother, who had changed into trousers before coming out, climbed over. Still slim and agile, she needed no more assistance than Jenny did.

Lucia too, despite the months of confinement with limited opportunities to exercise, was not so out of condition that she couldn't get over a gate. It was bad luck that she went over at the place where the top bar had been clouted by something heavy, perhaps by a piece of log-moving equipment. The impact had left the wood bruised and her hand was snagged by a splinter.

As they all walked on, she looked at the needle-sharp

fragment embedded in the heel of her hand with blood welling round it. She put it to her mouth to suck up the bright red fluid.

'What's the problem?' Suddenly Grey was walking beside her.

'No problem…just a small splinter.' He must be watching her like a hawk to have noticed.

'Let me see.' He took hold of her hand in his to examine it.

'It's nothing…I'll deal with it when we get back.'

'Better to deal with it now. Stand still.' Unnoticed by the others, he forced her to halt while he used both his thumbnails to prise the splinter from her flesh.

His nails were short and as clean as a doctor's or a vet's. But they felt like pincers and made her give a protesting, 'Ouch!'

Most men would have apologised, or stopped. Grey said, 'Bite the bullet,' and inflicted a few more seconds of minor agony on her before saying, 'It's out,' and showing her the half-inch splinter stuck to his bloody thumbnail before flicking it away.

Then, to her surprise and confusion, he began to suck the small wound.

The feel of his chinbone against the soft mound at the base of her thumb, the pressure of his lips and teeth and, most of all, the movements of his tongue as it swabbed away the blood, made her knees turn to jelly and her heart start to pound.

His hand was holding her wrist with the thumb close to her pulse. He must have felt the sudden acceleration. He had been looking at the ground, concentrating on what he was doing. Now his dark-lashed eyelids flicked up and his gaze met hers. For a moment they were expressionless, like a blank screen on a monitor. Then a message came into view. She could read it as easily as if it were lines of print.

He knew that what he was doing was exciting her, and the knowledge was exciting him.

Perhaps it was an automatic male reflex. To her chagrin, she felt her face beginning to change colour, a fiery glow spreading up from her neck to her forehead. She couldn't control her flush and nor could she look away.

The tension was broken by Jenny calling, 'What's up?' from where the other three had stopped to look back.

Grey moved Lucia's hand away from his mouth but kept hold of her wrist. 'Lucia picked up a splinter climbing the gate,' he called back.

The others began to retrace their steps. Lucia pulled her hand free and began walking towards them, feeling in her pocket for a tissue.

'It's nothing...it's out now,' she told them, hoping the flush had subsided.

'Is it bleeding?' asked Rosemary.

'Hardly at all,' said Lucia. But when she removed the tissue there was a speck of red on it and a small bead of blood on her skin.

'You need a patch on it,' said Rosemary. 'I always carry some in my walking trousers.'

She felt in her back pocket and produced two stretch fabric plasters in a transparent wrapper with a perforation down the middle.

Grey took it from her, tore one side off and opened it. His mother held out her hand to take the other plaster and the discarded wrapper while he peeled open the plaster's backing.

Lucia had no option but to wipe away the bead of

blood and hold her hand flat for him to apply the dressing.

'Thanks very much,' she said, speaking to his mother rather than to him.

'When did you last have a tetanus shot?' said Grey.

She wasn't sure that she had ever had one, certainly not since her schooldays. 'I don't know, but surely that isn't necessary. It's only a scratch.'

'A scratch can be dangerous,' said Mrs Calderwood. 'When Grey was at Cambridge, a friend of his scratched his arm on a rose bush growing beside some dustbins. Then he took a train to Scotland for a weekend with friends. By the time he arrived his whole arm was red and swollen. It was septicaemia…blood poisoning. If he hadn't been rushed to a doctor who pumped him full of anti-toxins, it could have been extremely serious…possibly fatal.'

'Better to be safe than sorry,' said Jenny. 'That was one thing I never had to worry about when the children were off on their travels. They were good about making sure they had all the important shots. Blood poisoning in the back of beyond is no joke.'

'I'll run you round to the doctor as soon as we get back,' said Grey.

'But it's Sunday,' she objected.

'He won't mind. He's a family friend.'

'George was angelically kind when my husband was ill,' said his mother. 'I saw him at church this morning. It won't take him two minutes, Lucia.'

'You've been outvoted,' said Tom, with a twinkle in his eyes. 'Take my advice and give in gracefully. When the Calderwoods come to a collective decision, they're an irresistible force. I speak from experience.'

'Tom likes to play at being hen-pecked,' said Jenny

good-humouredly. 'When it comes to the crunch, he's the boss and he knows it.'

'The crunch being what to do in an earthquake or a forest fire or some other unlikely scenario.'

The women laughed and Jenny feinted a punch at her husband's arm. Only Grey showed no amusement, Lucia noticed. He seemed to have switched off and be thinking his own thoughts.

When they returned to the house, Rosemary said, 'Braddy's gone out. Make some tea, would you, Jenny? I'll call George to ask if it's convenient for Grey to take Lucia round to him.'

An hour later, Lucia was sitting on a chair in the doctor's consulting room with her sleeve rolled up, waiting for him to inject her.

As if she were a small child who might need moral support, Grey had followed her in and was chatting to the elderly GP.

'There you are.' The doctor pressed a small pad over the skin the needle had punctured and told her to hold it in place. Some moments later he replaced the pad with a plaster. As he did so, he said, 'You're very pale, young lady. Not getting enough fresh air, by the look of you. Exercising in gyms is all very well, but a five-mile walk in the country is better. Take a leaf out of Grey's book. He's stuck in an office all week but he gets outside at weekends, don't you, Grey?'

'As often as I can. But I thought pale skins like Lucia's were back in fashion and the medical world was against getting outdoor tans.'

'Like everything else, it's a question of common sense. It's bad to get roasted by the sun, and women who sunbathe too much will undoubtedly wish they hadn't in thirty years' time when they're counting their wrinkles,' said the doctor. 'But being active in sunny weather is good for us.'

As he turned away to trash the disposable needle and empty serum container, Lucia mouthed, 'What about paying?'

Grey dismissed the question with a single shake of his head. Presently, after the doctor had walked with them to the car and waved them on their way, he said, 'You can go in and pay tomorrow when the office staff are there.'

'Have you known him all your life?'

'Yes, he came here about the same time as my parents. My sisters were born at Larchwood. When my father bought the house it was semi-derelict and going for the proverbial song. A lot of large houses were cheap when my parents were young because of the shortage of staff. He foresaw that central heating and other domestic appliances would make most of the manual labour unnecessary.'

Lucia had noticed that he always referred to 'my mother' and 'my father' instead of saying 'Mum' and 'Dad' as Jenny did. As his relationship with his mother was a close one, she concluded that this was a formality he used in talking to her, a way of keeping her at arm's length.

Yet the look in his eyes when he was sucking the small wound left by the splinter had been the reverse of aloof. It had been hot and hungry, as if it were months since he had been near a woman and she had done something deliberately provocative.

CHAPTER FIVE

ON THE short drive to the surgery neither of them had spoken and, although his car was a spacious one, she had been intensely aware of his tall frame alongside her and the lean brown hand that could so easily move from the gear lever to her thigh. Of course there was not the slightest chance that it would, but she had not been able to stop herself imagining how it would feel if it did.

No other man she had met, including those she had dated, had made her as physically conscious of her body, or his, as this man did. Considering that he and she had nothing in common, and a number of reasons for disliking each other, the attraction made no sense at all.

Making polite conversation, she said, 'Where were you born?'

'In a hospital in London. I was their last shot at having a son...though any one of my sisters could have carried on the business if I hadn't materialised.'

'Are you serious?'

'Certainly. If Jenny hadn't met Tom, she'd have ended up editing one of the nationals or a major provincial paper. They're all first-class forward planners and great delegators which is mainly what top management is about.'

'You said this morning that women were to blame for the breakdown of family life. What did you mean?'

'My nieces would tell you "Don't ask!"' he said dryly. 'At present they disapprove of my reactionary views, but they may change their minds when they're thirty-somethings and single mums, or wedded to their careers.'

'You don't approve of women having careers?' she asked, remembering what Rosemary had said about his father.

'On the contrary. The western world would collapse if they didn't.'

They had arrived at the entrance to Larchwood. He brought the car to a halt, waited for an oncoming car to pass, then drove through the gateway.

'But stable relationships are the bedrock of any successful culture. Take them away and you have chaos...children who get their ideas from TV instead of their parents...teenagers given lavish pocket money instead of parental attention...the whole disastrous breakdown of a sensible society.'

'And all that is women's fault?' said Lucia. 'Fathers are parents too.'

He drove past the side of the house and parked the car next to his brother-in-law's.

'Sure, but it was women who destroyed men's incentive to marry. For generations men married because that was the only way they could get regular sex. Then women started giving it away. What did they imagine would happen? I guess they thought they'd have fun and never mind the consequences.'

If prison had taught Lucia anything, it was to button her lip and stay out of trouble. At first it had gone against the grain to keep quiet when she wanted to argue or answer back. But, having seen what happened to people who did that, she had quickly learnt to lie low.

She said mildly, 'I could understand your father or grandfather taking that view. I'm surprised that you do.'

'Don't misunderstand me: I'm not saying a woman's place is in the home. If she has a brilliant brain and wants to use it...fine. That's her right. But it's been obvious for years that "having it all" isn't possible. If a man wants a good marriage, he knows he can't play the field the way he could when he was single. If a woman wants children, she should accept that a mother has obligations to be around when she's needed, which is for the first ten years. If she doesn't want to do that, she doesn't have to. It's one of life's choices.' He opened the driver's door and swung his long body out of the car.

Lucia stayed where she was, knowing that his training would oblige him to come round and open her door for her. Forcing him to accord her the courtesy he gave willingly to women he liked was a small way of venting her irritation at his dogmatic attitude. It wasn't his outlook that annoyed her as much as the way he expressed it...as if it were Holy Writ.

As he opened the door and she stepped out, she said, 'Aren't you ignoring the fact that even today a lot of children are conceived by chance rather than choice, and it's virtually impossible for a family to live on a single income?'

Grey leaned an arm on the top of the door. 'Not if they forget about keeping up with the Joneses. I have an elderly cleaner I don't often meet. She comes in when I'm out. I only got to know her when I was down with flu and she insisted on making me a huge pan of her special soup, and talking my ear off,' he added, with a faint smile. 'She brought up five children on her husband's pay as a milkman. Her daughter goes out to work to pay for designer trainers and other gear for the grandchildren, a fridge full of convenience foods and holidays abroad that involve long delays in airports and are more to impress the neighbours than for their enjoyment. As Mrs Botting says, "It don't make sense, Mr C." And she's right.'

Lucia was suddenly exhausted. Being alone with him was a strain she wasn't ready to handle yet. She said, 'A lot of things don't make sense. I expect it was always that way, and always will be. Thank you for taking me to the doctor.'

She walked quickly into the house and ran up the staircase, intending to stay in her room until all the visitors had gone.

An hour later she heard voices from the driveway and the sound of cars starting up and departing. Presently she went downstairs to find Mrs Calderwood in the drawing room working on a piece of needlepoint.

'What lovely colours,' she said, referring to the pile of embroidery wools in a cotton-lined shallow basket beside the older woman's chair.

'The design is a simplification of a photograph Grey took on one of his travels,' said Rosemary. 'Everything my mother worked was copied from an antique embroidery that had faded down to subdued shades. People forget—or don't realise—that all the needlework women did in past centuries would have been startlingly colourful when it was new. I wonder if your generation will do this sort of thing when they're older, or if there'll be quite different pastimes in forty years' time?'

'Who knows?' said Lucia vaguely. She still felt curiously drained by the hours in Grey's company. He stirred up emotions she didn't want to feel. Like someone just out of hospital, she needed a period of convalescence.

Rosemary said, 'Grey says you have some things in storage. We can retrieve them on Wednesday when we go to London for this architectural exhibition that Tom is so keen on us seeing. He was delighted by your interest in his hero, Alexander Thomson. Such a nice man, dear Tom. I'm very lucky in all my sons-in-law.'

She re-threaded her blunt-tipped needle with a strand of honey-coloured wool. 'But I think it's usually an easier relationship than with a daughter-in-law. Not that there's any sign of a daughter-in-law materialising. Grey's generation are wary of committing themselves. They have seen so many of their friends make mistakes that have led to ''being taken to the cleaners'' as he puts it.'

Lucia didn't want to talk about Grey. She said, 'What is the exhibition?'

'It's at the Royal Academy…a show of drawings by an eighteenth-century perspectivist. I'm sure we'll enjoy it, and afterwards they want us to have dinner with them. So we'll stay overnight with Grey. He has plenty of room.'

Lucia concealed her dismay at the thought of having to impose on Grey's unwilling hospitality. She said, 'It's very kind of you…and of Jenny and her husband…to include me in the invitation. But I don't think I should intrude in your family life more than is absolutely necessary. Perhaps, if you're going in the car, I could go to London with you, and then take the Underground to fetch my belongings and come back here by bus or train.'

'My dear, that would take you for ever. The village isn't well-served by public transport. Besides I want to be able to discuss the exhibition with you afterwards. Before we come home, we'll take in some other galleries and pick up inspiration for our first painting trip,' Rosemary said firmly.

When Lucia attempted to argue, she became even firmer. Lucia was reminded of the way she had told her son, 'From now on I shall do as *I* think best.'

It seemed she would have to fall in with Rosemary's wishes, however reluctantly. Unless Grey, when he was apprised of the plan, vetoed it. He might adamantly refuse to give houseroom to a jailbird, especially one whose crime had been damaging to him.

Returning to London in the black limousine with Rosemary was a more enjoyable experience than the outward journey when she had been mystified and uneasy. At least it was until Mrs Calderwood, who was reading the morning paper, turned the page and gave a smothered exclamation of surprise.

'Grey didn't tell me he'd been interviewed. I knew about the project, of course. I suppose it's bound to attract a lot of publicity.'

She held the page so that Lucia could read the headline across the top of it. 'Calderwood unveils plans for billion-pound office blocks.'

Below the headline were photographs of two huge ultra-modern buildings and, between them, superimposed, a photograph of Grey looking rather balefully down at the photographer who, judging from the perspective, must have been crouched below him.

'I'll read it and then let you have it,' said his mother.

A billion pounds was an unimaginable sum of money to Lucia. It made her even more nervous of the ordeal ahead. Larchwood was luxurious but it was also homely. What would his place be like? Even more luxurious and anything but homely, was how she imagined

it. Perhaps a million-pound penthouse on the fashionable Isle of Dogs, equipped with every gadget known
to electronics and stark minimalist furnishings chosen
by a top interior designer. Wherever it was, she knew
she would feel an interloper, a state of mind that Grey
might take pleasure in exacerbating.

It was several minutes before Rosemary detached a
sheet of four pages from the rest of the paper and passed
them to Lucia.

London is facing a space crunch with few buildings available to house large financial concerns.

This week Calderwood, the property company, unveils two of the biggest developments ever seen in
the City of London. Grey Calderwood, the group's
chief executive and grandson of the founder, has applied for planning permission to construct two showcase office buildings with a combined value of a billion pounds.

The piece went on to describe them in detail. It concluded:

Analysts say it will have a massive impact on
the group's net asset value. It is expected that
Calderwood will sell the buildings once they are
completed. It is likely they will both go to individual
occupiers who want a statement headquarters building.

'What do you think of them...as they're visualised?'
asked Rosemary, when Lucia folded the paper and put
it between them on the spacious back seat.

'I like this one the best,' said Lucia, pointing out the building marginally more pleasing to the eye than the other. Privately she thought them both eyesores, but perhaps it was impossible to make any building intended to house five thousand office workers look good to an artist's eye.

Rosemary made no comment. Perhaps she thought the same, but loyalty to her son kept her silent on the subject.

She said, 'Jackson is going to drop me off in Knightsbridge where I have some shopping to do. Then he'll take you to pick up your things and bring you to Grey's place. If I'm not there, he will be. He's working at home today.'

'What time do you expect to get there?' Lucia asked. The last thing she wanted was to show up on his doorstep before his mother's arrival.

'I'm not sure. I have quite a long list. Which reminds me…you will need some money. We haven't discussed your salary, but here is something on account.' She opened her bag, took out a sealed envelope and put it on Lucia's lap. 'Perhaps you have something in your luggage that is suitable to wear tonight, or you may want to buy something new. Do you like shopping for clothes? When my daughters were your age, they thought of nothing else.'

'Before Dad was ill, I spent most of my salary on painting things and books about art,' said Lucia. 'I had a few good clothes for work and the rest of the time I wore trousers and T-shirts. Will a silk shirt and a black skirt be all right for tonight?'

'Perfect,' Rosemary assured her.

*   *   *

At that moment Grey was standing, naked, in his bathroom, shaving.

Normally he was an early riser, arriving in his office a couple of hours before his staff began their day. But he had been working until the small hours and was up late because he needed at least six hours' sleep to recharge his batteries.

The mirror behind the white washbasin set in a black marble counter reflected a torso that being naturally olive-skinned, and regularly exposed to the sun during the brief 'escapes' that followed most of his business trips, never lost its light amber tan.

The movements of his right arm, as he drew the razor over the taut skin that covered the clearly defined bone structure of his face, indicated that between his shoulder and wrist there were powerful muscles that, if exerted more strenuously, would swell to a formidable size.

His chest, too, was that of a man as active physically as he was mentally, his midriff and stomach still as hard as they had been ten years earlier in his middle twenties. This was not because he was ascetic in his habits, never indulging in expensive lunches in London's leading restaurants. But when he attended such occasions, he was selective in his choices from the menu and, though he never declined the vintage wines that accompanied the gourmet food, he drank rather less than his corpulent, high-complexioned, jowly colleagues.

As one journalist, specialising in profiles of top businessmen, had written of him:

The term 'fat-cat industralist' can never be applied to Grey Calderwood. Images of the cat family do come to mind when talking to him, but they are of other felines; lions, leopards and cheetahs. Although urbane in manner and, according to several women I spoke to, a charmer when he chooses, Calderwood, like the late newspaper tycoon, Lord Beaverbrook, is 'the cat that walks alone'.

From the hips down, Grey's body was hidden from the mirror by the counter. But he wasn't studying his reflection. He was thinking, with extreme displeasure, about the arrival of 'that bloody girl' as he had mentally tagged Lucia.

He liked having his mother using his home as her London base. He liked taking her to places where a woman of her age wouldn't normally go, such as the popular Japanese restaurant where everyone sat on benches at long refectory-style tables and most people chatted to their neighbours as well as to the person they were with. He sometimes went there on his own. The young who frequented it kept him in touch with the world of crowded commuter trains, money worries and other realities of life from which he himself was free. Which was not to say he didn't have burdens of his own, no less onerous for not being the common causes of stress.

He finished shaving, bent to sluice his face with cold water, then stepped into the shower compartment, closed the glass door and reached for a tube of shampoo. Washing his hair, as he did every morning, he tried to erase from his mind the irritation of having to play host to that girl.

It was an impossible situation. His mother was determined to befriend her and he was equally determined to get shot of her. But how?

Even Jenny, whom he had hoped would support him,

had taken to the girl. Jenny seemed to find the situation amusing rather than annoying. But then all his sisters had always had a perverse sense of humour.

The insights he had gleaned from them about the workings of the female mind should have put him off women for life. It hadn't. But it had made him wary of the so-called weaker sex. The truth was that most women were ten times as tough as men. If it were not for their biology, and the limitations it imposed on them, they would have been running the world since the dawn of time.

After lathering the rest of his body, he turned on the power-shower and closed his eyes against the downpour of warm water. The first hot shower of the day—he usually had another in the evening when he got back from the office—was a pleasure he took time to enjoy, in the same way that he relished a good breakfast.

This morning his enjoyment was marred by the memory of that girl lying full-length in the bath at Larchwood. Tonight, she would be using the shower in one of his guest rooms. As he thought of her nude figure standing in the steamy warmth of an identical glass cubicle, his annoyance was exacerbated by finding his body responding to the mental image. He could visualise her sleek wet skin, her head thrown back in the attitude of a woman surrendering to a sensual experience.

As his erection intensified, so did his anger. Cursing, he changed the shower's setting, hoping the deluge of cold water would rapidly kill off his unwanted ardour. Maddeningly, it didn't. His over-heated imagination now presented him with another scenario: the two of them sharing this shower, her mouth and body warm against his despite the cold raining down on them.

And then it came to him…a sure-fire way to get rid of her. All he had to do was to make a heavy pass. That would change her mind about staying.

It had been obvious, when he was dealing with the splinter in her hand on Sunday, that she disliked being touched by him. She would dislike it even more if, tonight, after his mother had gone to bed, he started coming on strong.

He turned off the shower, opened the door and reached for the white towelling robe on a hook within reach.

On the way back from Larchwood at the weekend, he realised it had been an act of thoughtless stupidity to suck a puncture on the hand of a woman who, for all he knew, might be as promiscuous as they came. How did he know how many men she had slept with or who they might have had sex with?

Once before he had taken a similar risk. But the circumstances had been different. Driving on an empty road, he had stopped at the scene of an accident that had taken place minutes before. The occupants of both cars had been seriously injured. He had called for help on his mobile, then done what he could until the professionals arrived.

It had involved mouth-to-mouth resuscitation, and getting blood on his hands. Just for a couple of seconds before wading in, he had hesitated, aware of the dangers inherent in body fluids. It had been a moment of decision: a contest between the promptings of humanity and the instinct for self-preservation. Humanity had won, and later he'd had the satisfaction of knowing that his first aid had made the difference between survival or death for the most seriously injured casualty.

Nowadays he kept in his car rubber gloves and a

gadget that allowed resuscitation without physical contact. They were sensible precautions in today's world. Caution hadn't crossed his mind on Sunday afternoon. He had forgotten that she was fresh out of prison and that he had many reasons to dislike her. A lifetime of training in the behaviour his mother and sisters considered the proper function of the male had kicked in, overriding the guardedness and cynicism he had learned in a cut-throat business world.

It was an error of judgment he wouldn't make a second time.

'Why have we come here?' Lucia asked Jackson when, shortly before one o'clock, he opened the door for her to step out of the car.

The limousine was parked within yards of the River Thames, near a small marina with Venetian-style striped posts marking the moorings.

'This is where Mr Grey lives, miss,' said the chauffeur. 'In the Thames lighter over there.' He pointed towards a two-storey barge at the far end of the pontoon walkway that gave access to the various craft berthed on either side of it.

'There?' Lucia echoed, astonished. 'Do you mean all the time? All year round?'

'Yes, miss,' Jackson said impassively. 'If you'd like to go ahead, I won't be long bringing your things.'

CHAPTER SIX

LUCIA walked slowly in the direction he indicated, trying to adjust to the fact that Grey's living quarters were so different from her preconceptions. Why on earth would a man at the head of a company whose stock-market value had made her blink as she read it live in a place like this?

Not that it wasn't a lovely place to live...by her standards. The breeze coming off the water, the wide expanse of river stretching away in both directions, the sense of space and freedom in the middle of one of the world's great cities; all these appealed to her strongly. But it seemed an unlikely environment for Grey and his collection of expensive paintings to inhabit.

She was wearing flat rubber-soled shoes that made no sound on the planking but, as she approached the lighter, which she knew was the name for a flat-bottomed barge used for transporting cargo when ships were being loaded or unloaded, Grey appeared on the covered deck that seemed to run right round the vessel.

'Good morning. Come aboard,' he said. He did not go as far as to smile at her, but his manner was not unwelcoming.

'Good morning. Is your mother here?' she asked hopefully.

'Not yet.' He looked past her to where Jackson was following with her cases. 'Are those all your worldly goods, or only some of them?'

'Everything. Mrs Calderwood persuaded me to col-

lect both cases. She said there was no point in leaving
the second one in storage when she has plenty of attic
space.' She did not use his mother's first name sensing
that, even though she had been given permission to do
so, he would think it presumptuous.

'There's not much point in having them on board
overnight, Jackson. Put them back in the car and take
them to Larchwood. You'll need some lunch before you
go back. Have the meal of the day at the Crown and
Anchor. It's usually excellent. Tell them to chalk it up
to me.'

'Thank you, sir.'

Jackson went back the way he had come.

'It's useful having a good pub nearby,' said Grey. 'I
expect you'd like to wash your hands before lunch. I'll
show you your quarters.'

Although the exterior of the barge made it clear that
the interior would be a lot more roomy than the between
decks accommodation on most boats, Lucia was unpre-
pared for the spaciousness of the huge living room with
its panoramic views of the river. It even had a large
fireplace, she noticed with surprise.

At one end of the living room was an immaculate
kitchen with a breakfast bar.

'This deck is fifty feet long by sixteen feet wide so
I'm not cramped for space,' said Grey, leading the way.

To her annoyance, Lucia found herself eyeing the
broad shoulders and sexy male backside that had already caught her eye on Sunday's walk, more interested
in his vital statistics than the boat's.

Frowning, she asked, 'How long have you lived
here?'

'Since the development the marina belongs to was
completed four years ago.'

She hadn't paid much attention to the buildings along the riverbank. They must be another valuable Calderwood development.

'We were reading about your latest project in the paper on the way here,' she said.

Grey made no comment. He was moving fast down a short flight of metal stairs leading to a lower deck. Lucia followed, reminded of wider and longer metal staircases between narrow landings ranged with rows of cells.

Built in Victorian times, the prison had offered little scope for modernisation beyond lighter paintwork and some improvement in the sanitation. A shiver went through her. Would she always be haunted by the memory of those months 'inside'?

Grey opened a door leading into a room with twin bunks, one above the other. This, too, was a reminder of sharing a cell with a woman who, for their first three days together, had looked as if she would like to murder Lucia and might have a sudden brainstorm and do it.

'This is where I sometimes put up my nephews and nieces when their parents want a short respite,' said Grey. His tone was faintly sardonic, suggesting that he didn't mind relieving his sisters of their offspring occasionally, but was not in the market for such domestic responsibilities himself.

'There's a shower through there,' he added, pointing out a door in the wall opposite the bunks. 'I think you'll find everything you need. Come up to the living room when you're ready and we'll have a drink.'

'It looks very comfortable. Thank you.'

'My pleasure.' The look he gave her before closing the door after him didn't match the polite response to her thanks.

For some moments after he had gone she stood staring at the coat hooks on the back of the door, trying to analyse the curious glint in those usually enigmatic dark grey eyes. In the antagonistic context of their relationship to date, her conclusion didn't make sense.

She had to be mistaken. It must have been a trick of the light reflected off the river whose soft plashing against the hull she could hear through the half-open window.

Yet, for a moment, she could have sworn that Grey was looking at her like a man with sex on his mind.

On her way back to the upper deck, her attention was caught by a painting of a rectangular pool seen from one end with arches at the other and sunlight suffusing the air. There was nothing to indicate where the place was or who had painted the original. Somewhere in southern Europe, was her guess.

Grey was watching the river when she joined him.

'Is white wine all right for you?' he asked, swinging round and appraising the cream cotton shirt previously concealed by her light all-purpose raincoat. Or was he mentally undressing her?

Wishing his mother would arrive, she told herself that she *must* be imagining that his attitude towards her had undergone a drastic change.

While he took a bottle with a French label from a transparent plastic cooler and began filling a glass, she asked, 'Is the painting on the staircase wall a souvenir of a holiday?'

His response was not the momentarily blank look of someone who can't remember what they have on their walls because they have stopped looking at them.

He said instantly, 'In a manner of speaking. Did you recognise it? Have you been there?'

Lucia shook her head. 'Where is it?'

Grey handed her a glass. 'It's one of the courtyards in the Alhambra palace in Granada...the last stronghold of the Muslim kings of Granada before they were driven out at the end of the fifteenth century. I spent part of my gap year, between school and university, exploring Spain and learning the language. Did you have a gap year?'

'No, I went straight from school to art college.' As soon as she had spoken, she wished she had just said no. The mention of her art training must remind him of matters she wanted to put behind her. Not that he was ever likely to forget them, but at least he seemed willing to put them aside for the time being.

Replacing the bottle in the cooler and picking up his own glass, he gestured for her to choose somewhere to sit. 'If it's possible,' he said, 'I think a gap year is a valuable interval between school and higher education. Often it can change people's ideas about how they want to spend their lives...open their minds to the fact that other cultures have different, equally valid, ways of doing things.'

'Did you like the Spanish culture? Is it very different from ours?'

'Yes to both questions. But it's probably changed a lot in the eighteen years since I was there. I've never been back. For various reasons, it's not one of the countries where the company has been involved in developments. But because of Spain's once-vast empire, the language is useful in other parts of the world.'

Lucia would have seated herself in one of the chairs, but before she could sit down he hooked a hand through the crook of her elbow, saying, 'No, sit on the sofa where you can see the river.'

There was no way she could refuse, even though every instinct told her it wasn't a good idea to sit where there was space for Grey to sit beside her. To her relief he didn't. He moved away to open a cupboard. Moments later, still holding his glass in his right hand, he returned to the long low table placed in front of the sofa with a small earthenware dish and a vacuum-sealed foil pack in his other hand. Placing glass and dish on the table, he opened the pack and shook its contents—cashew nuts—into the dish.

The shape of his hands made her long for pencil and drawing pad. The form and structure of the male body had always appealed to her more than the curves of the female figure. For her generation of students, life classes, to her regret, had not been part of the curriculum. But she had taken every opportunity to draw people and filled sketchbooks with studies of hands from the fat starfish fingers of babies to the arthritis-twisted hands of the old.

Between those two extremes were these beautiful, powerful hands she was watching now as he made a missile of the pack by twisting it into a knot and took accurate aim at a nearby wastepaper basket. Then he offered the dish of nuts to her.

'Thank you.' Lucia helped herself to a couple.

Then he joined her on the sofa and any hope of relaxing and enjoying the view, the wine and the salty taste of the cashews immediately evaporated. Especially as he didn't settle himself at the other end of the three-seater sofa but on the central section, with his body angled towards her and his elbow on top of the backrest so that his hand dangled between them.

She had already noticed that, unlike most of the top-level businessmen she had seen on TV or in real life, he did not wear a signet ring on his little finger. Nor was his watch one of the well-known status symbols of those who were rich and liked everyone to know it. Even his casual clothes were non-conformist. His shirt didn't advertise, even discreetly, that it was from the collection of a famous designer. His pants were the kind of chinos that could be found in any street market. Clearly, he didn't need anything to boost or reinforce his innate self-confidence. In a way she liked that. As long as it didn't lead to arrogance.

'What's that bridge in the distance?' she asked.

'Wandsworth Bridge. One of the advantages of this mooring is it's close to Battersea heliport. My father went everywhere by road and rail, but the roads weren't such a snarl-up in his time. A helicopter is the only way to get out of the city quickly. I like driving and I generally use the car to get to Larchwood, but mostly I fly.'

'Do you mean you fly yourself, or have someone to fly you?'

'I fly myself. It's not difficult…no more so than driving a car. Do you drive?'

'My father taught me when I was in my teens and I passed the test. But I've hardly ever used my licence. After his old car failed its road test, it was more economical to use public transport than to replace it. At my last job, as long as we did the work we could go in early or stay late to avoid travelling in the rush hours.'

'That was a sensible policy. The way things are heading, I see more and more people working from home or returning to the inner cities to live. For millions of people to spend hours of their lives commuting is a huge waste of life. If I— He broke off to point out a river police launch moving downstream.

When, as it passed out of sight, he did not complete his unfinished remark but switched to the subject of river traffic, Lucia had the feeling that the launch's appearance had been a timely pretext to cut off a train of thought he had realised he did not wish to share with her.

Forgetting for a moment the invidious nature of her situation in his family circle, she said, 'But if you think that, why isn't your company building inner city housing developments instead of huge office blocks that can only add to the commuter traffic?'

She saw the muscles at the angle of his jaw tighten, perhaps with annoyance, but his tone was even as he said, 'Planning permissions take a long time to go through. From concept to realisation is a matter of years, not months. They may be the last such blocks we do build.'

He leaned forward to pick up the dish of cashews and offer it to her. When he replaced it and sat back, the space between them had diminished and now his arm was stretched along the backrest behind her shoulders.

If he had been any other man, Lucia would have felt certain that his next move would be to take her in his arms. But she couldn't bring herself to believe that this was Grey's intention. It didn't make sense. Less than ten days ago he had hated her guts, offered a large sum of money to get her out of their lives. If she had been incredibly beautiful or sexy-looking, it was just conceivable that he might have changed his mind...men being notoriously prone to testosterone-fuelled impulses. But she wasn't either beautiful or sexy.

A number of men had made passes at her in the past,

but then any reasonably presentable female had had that experience. They had mostly been middle-aged office Romeos or callow youths hoping she might be more compliant than the gorgeous girls they really wanted but couldn't pull. Grey didn't come into either of those categories. With his looks, money and position he could pretty well take his pick. So why would he bother with her?

Unless... Struck by a possibility that was a bit far-fetched but not impossible, she took a swig of her wine. Maybe, just maybe he was swine enough to think that a pass was a cheaper and more effective way to get rid of her than his previous gambit.

On the point of jumping up and putting as much space between them as was possible without the reason becoming too obvious, she had a better idea. Filed away in her memory was a tip she had picked up at art school from the kind of girl who had men pursuing her in droves.

'When they start coming on strong and I don't want to play, I reach for the nearest food,' luscious blonde Katie had said. 'They can't kiss you with your mouth full.'

'But what if there isn't any food?' another girl had asked her.

'There always is...if you keep a choc bar in your bag. It's amazing how long you can make half a choc bar last if you really need to,' Katie had said, with a giggle.

Lucia leaned forward and scooped up a handful of nuts. 'These are terribly more-ish, aren't they?' she said, putting several in her mouth.

It worked like a charm. Grey drained his wineglass and rose to his feet. Fetching the bottle he refilled his own and topped up hers, saying, 'You're obviously hungry. We won't wait lunch for my mother. She may have got held up shopping. She loves buying presents for her grandchildren.'

'How many grandchildren are there?'

'Eight. Jenny, whom you've met, and Julia my eldest sister, have two each. Lolly, the youngest of the three, has four. She and her husband are doctors. They always seem to have larger than average families. I'll get some food organised.'

'Can I do anything to help?'

'No, thanks, it's all organised. Stay where you are and enjoy those more-ish nuts.'

Was there a gleam of mockery in his glance before he turned away? Did he guess why she had suddenly gone into starving squirrel mode?

Grey *had* guessed. He had been reading female body language for a long time and, although it wasn't usual for women to show signs of alarm when he was sitting close to them, Lucia had been signalling her nervousness for some minutes before stuffing the nuts in her mouth.

Actually it had not been his intention to make his move when, at any moment, they might be joined by his mother. He had merely been playing cat and mouse, deriving a somewhat sadistic satisfaction from watching her react to her reading of the situation.

Earlier, he had narrowly stopped himself from telling her something he had never discussed with anyone. Why he should even think of making her his confidante was beyond him. She was the last person in the world he would trust with his private concerns.

It had also annoyed him when Lucia had had the nerve to tell him what the company should be doing.

She seemed to have very little sense of the insecurity of her position. She was the sort who, given an inch, would always take a mile, he thought sourly.

But his mind was too analytical not to be aware that part of his annoyance was directed at himself. The fact was that although the object of tonight's exercise was to get rid of her, he felt no reluctance at putting the plan into practice but rather anticipation.

He wanted to know how her body would feel in his arms, how her mouth would feel under his. Though of course the last thing he wanted was a willing response. The more outraged she was the better.

As he moved about the stainless steel and cherry-wood kitchen, making the final preparations for the meal prepared by his home help, Mrs Botting, he remembered a scandal a couple of years ago when a girl in Calderwood's Birmingham office had accused the manager of her department of sexual harassment. Grey had prevailed on her to change her mind by dismissing the man involved. He had not been a satisfactory employee on a number of accounts. Satisfied that the girl had done nothing to provoke the manager, Grey had sympathised with her. He could understand the distress it must cause to have to cope with a middle-aged groper on a daily basis.

But he had no compunction about making a pass at Lucia. Every instinct told him she would resist. There was no question of them ending up in bed together. Nor was there any likelihood of her screaming for a lawyer.

CHAPTER SEVEN

IN HER art student days, and later when she was working at the advertising agency, Lucia had often passed through the great triple archway leading off the north side of Piccadilly on her way to the loan exhibitions put on by the Royal Academy.

The spacious courtyard surrounding the statue of Sir Joshua Reynolds, the Academy's first president, with his palette in one hand and a paintbrush in the other, was the scene of many happy memories for her. Here, with her fellow students, she had stood in line to see masterpieces by Goya, Tiepolo and other immortal artists.

Life had seemed full of promise then. Even after the realities of earning a living had forced her to recognise her limitations and modify her ambitions, there had still been the golden dream of meeting her true love to make life seem an exciting adventure.

That prospect, too, was tarnished now; partly by her own fault, and partly by the experience of people she knew whose dreams of being happy-ever-after had ended in disillusionment.

Tonight, crossing the courtyard in the company of Rosemary and her son, Lucia remembered the other occasions when she had come here. This time her sense of anticipation was counterbalanced by apprehension. Although it was most unlikely she would be recognised, it was hard to rid herself of the feeling that what she had done, and where she had been, hung about her like an inescapable aura.

The others were waiting for them by the steps to the entrance and soon they were all in the crowded foyer dominated by a majestically wide staircase leading up to the lofty galleries.

For some reason the crush in the foyer made Lucia feel uncomfortable to the point of wanting to turn tail. But escape was an impossibility. She just had to tough it out until her uneasiness passed off.

Grey was at an advantage in crowded places, his height allowing him to see beyond the people surrounding him. But tonight he was not looking out for people he knew and would be expected to speak to. Social obligations—never of primary importance to him—were the last thing on his mind. He had other fish to fry.

He glanced at the fish in question, forced to acknowledge that she was looking unexpectedly striking in her cream silk shirt and a long narrow black skirt that looked decorous when she was standing still but gave eye-catching glimpses of her slim legs when she moved.

Without any jewellery and with only minimal make-up, somehow she managed to outshine most of the women present despite their designer outfits and hours spent at expensive hairdressers. The sheer black tights she was wearing had been a present from his mother when she returned from her shopping expedition.

Looking at Lucia more closely, he noticed a faint sheen of moisture on her temples. Although the foyer was crowded, the temperature was not uncomfortably high even for men in suits and certainly not for women. The dew on her skin had to be caused by some form of stress.

Her discomfiture should have left him unmoved, even pleased him. But he found that it didn't.

In a murmured aside the others wouldn't catch, he said, 'Are you feeling ill? Do you need to get out of here?'

Lucia was amazed that, of the four people she was with, it should be Grey who recognised her unease and offered assistance. For an instant she caught herself thinking what a rock of support the man would be to a woman he cared about.

Then she realised his concern was not really for her but rather for the rest of the party who would have their enjoyment disrupted if, as he might fear, she fainted or threw up.

She pinned a bright smile to her lips. 'I'm feeling fine,' she assured him. Then, seeing his face harden, would have added, But thank you for your concern, if his sister hadn't chosen that moment to speak to him.

Once they had mounted the staircase and were being led round the exhibition by Tom, the panicky feelings subsided. She was able to give most of her mind to what they had come to see. But, interesting as the exhibition was, it could not wholly distract her from her puzzlement over Grey who, at times, showed signs of detesting her, this afternoon had seemed as if he might pounce, and a little while ago had tuned in to her unease more intuitively than either his mother or sister.

The man was a conundrum. Would she ever understand what made him tick? Sometimes she had the feeling that even the people closest to him didn't really know him.

A week later Grey drove down to Larchwood. Since the night of the Academy party he had been annoyed with himself for not carrying out his intention to get rid of Lucia by making a heavy pass.

But, when it came to the point, he had changed his mind. Aware that the evening had already been some kind of ordeal for her, he had found himself curiously reluctant to add to her problems.

In the meantime he had thought of a more orthodox way of discouraging her.

Lucia was alone in the house when Grey arrived. Both Rosemary and Braddy were out, visiting a former home help who was recovering from an operation.

After she had offered him coffee, which he declined, Grey said, 'Before you start driving my mother around on these painting trips, I'd like to satisfy myself that you're a competent driver. You can show off your paces in my car.' He handed her the keys.

Lucia was appalled. Driving a strange car—a very expensive car—with Grey watching her every move was an ordeal she wasn't ready for. For a moment she was tempted to say, I can't...you will make me too nervous. Then she realised she had no option. If she chickened out, he would use it as a lever to get rid of her. He had backed off last time, when his mother had stood her ground on the day of Lucia's arrival. But he wouldn't do that a second time.

'Do you think that's a fair test? Your car isn't exactly typical of the average hired car,' she pointed out.

'A competent driver should be able to drive anything short of a heavy goods vehicle,' he said sternly. 'I'm not asking you to take it into a maelstrom of traffic. The roads around here are quiet.'

As they walked towards his car, Lucia remembered

her official driving test. She had been nervous, but nothing like as nervous as she was now. The examiner had been a small balding man whose manner had been pleasant if not exactly friendly. But he certainly hadn't been hostile, as she felt Grey was. He *wanted* her to fail. She could feel it in her bones.

He was so determined to get rid of her that he was prepared to risk damage to his beautiful car in order to achieve that end.

Gritting her teeth, she gathered her will-power together, determined to stay cool and not let him throw her into a panic.

Grey opened the driver's door for her. 'You'll need to adjust the seat. I'll show you how in a moment.' He closed the door and walked round the bonnet.

The interior of the car had the luxurious smell of real leather upholstery, but she wasn't in the mood to appreciate it, or the elegant arrangement of the various dials on the custom-built walnut fascia. Part of her felt as daunted as if she were sitting in the cockpit of a private plane.

Grey slid his tall frame into the passenger seat and closed them inside what suddenly seemed a much smaller space than it had when she was occupying it by herself.

Having shown her how to adjust the seat, he then pointed out all the controls.

Finally he sat back, pulled the seat-belt across his shoulder and chest, clipped it into place and said, 'Right: it's all yours.'

Forty minutes later, she drove back up the drive, feeling as if she had been through a gruelling three-day course to test her mental and physical stamina.

After she had stopped the car, put on the handbrake and switched off the engine, she turned and looked him in the eyes. 'Are you satisfied?'

'You seem to be competent…in not very testing conditions,' he tacked on.

Lucia removed the keys from the ignition and handed them to him. His grudging agreement infuriated her. There had been a couple of moments when, if she hadn't anticipated poor road use on the part of other drivers, his car might have been damaged. He had to have nerves of steel to have sat through those two incidents without showing any sign of wanting to grab the wheel or even of being on edge. But while his self-control might be admirable, she could not admire his unwillingness to concede how well she had performed, given the nature of the test.

'You hoped I would fail, didn't you?' she said bluntly. 'You still want me out of here'—with a gesture embracing Larchwood.

As if he intended to ignore the question, Grey got out of the car. Expecting him to head for the front door, she stayed where she was, her hands clenched with rage at the cold arrogance of the man.

Instead, to her surprise, he came round to open her door. Resting one arm along the top of it, he looked down at her with an expression she could not read. 'I expected you to fail,' he said coolly. 'But the stakes were high and you rose to the occasion. I admire your ability to do that. Just be sure that you maintain the same level of care when you're driving my mother.'

It took all Lucia's self-control not to tell him she had never met a more monumental prig. In fact the epithet on the tip of her tongue was even more derogatory. As she bit it back, she could tell by the gleam in his eye that he knew what was in her mind and had been deliberately goading her to say something he could use against her.

Swinging her legs out of the car, she put her feet to the ground, stood up and said, with saccharine politeness, 'I'll do my best, I promise you.'

The memory of his attempt to expel her from the Calderwood orbit was something she thought about every time she and his mother used the car they had rented to explore the narrow lanes and winding coastal roads on the little island of Guernsey, a dependency of the British Crown but closer to the coast of France.

'I wish Grey would pop over and join us for a couple of days,' said Rosemary, more than once during their stay.

Lucia murmured agreement but hoped that he wouldn't. She had fallen in love with the place and didn't want her pleasure marred by Grey's disturbing presence.

They were lucky with the weather and spent long hours out of doors, painting.

'You are looking *much* better,' Rosemary told her, the day they flew back to the mainland. 'Being here has done you good.'

The success of their first painting trip made Rosemary eager to venture further afield. She knew of a house in Spain that some friends had rented for their summer holiday, describing its setting as idyllic.

On the evening that the long range forecast on TV said a month of wet weather was ahead, she rang the owners of the house at their English number and ar-

ranged to take it for a week with an option to extend
the booking if she wished.

The following morning she called a travel agency in
the nearest town and asked them to organise two first-
class seats on a scheduled flight to Alicante.

Grey heard about this development when he came to
Larchwood at the weekend to be present at a dinner
party Rosemary had set up some time ago as part of a
neighbour's programme to entertain a VIP house guest.

'I planned the table before it was certain you would
be here,' she told Lucia. 'I hope you won't mind being
left out?'

'Of course not,' Lucia assured her. 'I don't expect to
be included in everything. If I may, I'll spend the evening reading your new guidebooks.' A parcel of books
had arrived from London that morning.

Grey arrived a couple of hours before the others were
due. He looked rather worn, Lucia thought, as he entered the drawing room. As if, even at the summit of
the Calderwood organisation, it had been a tough week.

Each time she saw him, he struck her as too physical
a man to spend his life behind a desk, or at the head of
the table in a boardroom. On the bridge of a naval ship,
or in charge of an army command post—yes. She could
visualise him in any number of jobs from war-reporting
on TV to conducting important million-dollar sales for
a leading fine arts auction house. But he didn't seem to
fit what he really did. His height, his shoulders, his bear-
ing and especially his angular jawline and hard midriff
were not those of any top echelon businessmen she had
ever seen.

After greeting them both, he kissed his mother and
went to fix himself a drink. 'What about you two?' he
asked, opening the corner cupboard.

'Not for me, dear. Lucia, would you like something?'

'No, thanks.' Lucia found it hard not to watch him. He seemed to draw her gaze to him, like a pin being drawn to a magnet.

Their forthcoming trip to Spain came up a few minutes later when Grey mentioned a film opening in London the following week. 'I think you'd enjoy it. It's a romantic comedy.'

'I'm sure we should, but we'll have to see it some other time,' said Rosemary, going on to explain why next week was not possible.

Lucia expected to see one of Grey's forbidding frowns appear and was surprised when he received the news impassively.

When Rosemary said it was time she went up to change, Lucia left the room with her.

About forty minutes later, she was reading one of the guidebooks when there was a knock on her door. She knew it wasn't Rosemary or Braddy. There was only one person it could be, though why he should come to her room she couldn't imagine.

'Come in.'

As he opened the door, she laid down the book, reminded of the day he had burst into the bathroom. The memory warmed her cheeks and she hoped the colour didn't show.

'Would you like a drink now?' he asked.

'It's kind of you...but I think I'll stay on water tonight.' She indicated the bottle of mineral water on the table beside her armchair.

The bedroom had another armchair on the far side of the dressing table but she hesitated to ask him to sit down. If his brother-in-law had had a reason to enter her room, it wouldn't have made her feel on edge. But, apart from being a loving husband, Tom was a different kind of man. The sort women instinctively felt safe with. She couldn't imagine ever feeling safe with Grey, at least not in the sense of being unaware of his masculinity and seeing him simply as another human being.

'Are you happy about this Spanish trip?' he asked. 'There could be language difficulties...and driving on the right can be tricky, the first time you do it.'

'I don't have a problem with it. Do you?' she asked bluntly.

It must have been fifteen seconds before he answered. The long pause increased her tension.

Finally, he said, 'Not provided you give me your word to make immediate contact if anything should go wrong.'

'Of course you have my word on that.' It had to be a step forward that he thought her word was worth having.

'Good.' Turning back to the door, he paused. 'By the way, you're not missing anything. If the visiting senator is anything like his English cousins, it will be an extremely dull evening. You're better off up here. Goodnight, Lucia.'

'Goodnight.' His use of her name sent a strange tremor through her.

As the door closed behind him, she relaxed. She took up the book and tried to focus on details that might be useful when they reached Spain. But in her mind's eye she saw the tall figure going down the stairs, a dutiful son taking his late father's place and supporting his mother through an evening not of his choosing.

Behind the sometimes urbane, sometimes autocratic façade, what was he really like?

CHAPTER EIGHT

COCOONED in the comfortable tranquillity of the first-class section of the aircraft taking them to Spain, Rosemary and Lucia were sipping the drinks offered to them within moments of their being seated, and flipping through their copies of the airline's in-flight magazines, when a stewardess said, 'Here you are, sir,' and made a gracious gesture at the two empty seats on the other side of the aisle.

'Grey!' his mother exclaimed, when she saw who the newcomer was. 'What are you doing here?'

'I'm taking a few days off. You don't mind if I join you, do you?' His glance at Lucia included her in the question.

'What a lovely surprise,' said Rosemary, answering for both of them. 'But why spring it on us like this? If you'd let us know last night, we could have collected you on the way here.'

'It was possible I might have had to pull out at the last moment.'

'Shall I help you with your things, sir?' the stewardess offered, opening the overhead locker.

'I can manage, thanks.'

Watching them, Lucia thought the girl might as well have been a steward for all the notice he took of her. The immaculately lipsticked mouth maintained its smile, but Lucia knew she was piqued by his total in-difference to her considerable charms. What would it take to make him exert *his* charm? Obviously more than Miss World looks.

Another stewardess materialised. 'A drink for you, sir?'

'Thank you. The same as these ladies, please.'

As he finished arranging his belongings, Lucia recovered from the shock of his arrival. She stood up. 'Let me sit there and you sit here.'

'No, no—you're fine where you are.'

He placed his hands on her shoulders to make her sit down. It was a light casual gesture that had an effect far beyond what he intended. The brief pressure of his palms and fingertips set up a frisson that went all the way to her toes.

Shaken, she resumed her seat and Grey sat down alongside her, the generous seating space allowing even his long legs to stretch out in comfort.

'Now we can really relax,' Rosemary murmured happily, her aside not intended for her son's ears. 'If there are any complications, Grey can handle them.'

Lucia managed to smile, but it wasn't the way she felt about his arrival. She had been more relaxed before he showed up. Now the pleasure of her first visit to Spain was going to be tempered by the feeling of being under critical scrutiny.

Finding the village wasn't difficult. Finding the house, without Grey to ask directions, would have been. It was in a narrow street and, from outside, did not look anything to write home about, all its windows shuttered, its front door screened by a plastic blind.

Grey had to roll this up out of the way before he could unlock the door. The two women entered a dark hall with several doors leading off it. The one Rosemary opened led into a large kitchen with, only dimly visible, a small window on the street side and another taller window at the other end.

While Rosemary dealt with the shutters at the window above the sink, Lucia went to draw the long cotton curtains screening the second window. They hung from a wooden rail close to the ceiling and their hems almost touched the clay-tiled floor.

Parting the curtains did not admit any light because outside the glass was a blind similar to the one on the front door. She was trying to fathom how to raise it when Grey came up behind her and located a length of strong tape hidden by the right-hand curtain. But when he pulled on it, the blind didn't budge. He then opened one of the sliding glass panes, disturbing a scuttle of small spiders, and undid a couple of screws half hidden by cobwebs that were holding the blind in place.

The scene now exposed to view made Lucia give a small gasp of pleasure. Outside was a narrow railed terrace and beyond it, at a lower level, a courtyard about the size of a tennis court. Its walls were covered with creepers and just visible above the top of one wall were the Roman-tiled roofs of the house in another street on a much lower level than the one outside No 12. Beyond the mellow old rooftops could be seen a large expanse of vineyards and, beyond them, a range of mountains.

'Can't fault the outlook,' said Grey, bringing her back to a sharp awareness of how close together they were standing. Then he moved away. 'What's behind here, I wonder?'

She turned to find him releasing the brass catches holding a pair of folding doors in place.

'What an unusual ceiling,' said Rosemary, making Lucia look up at the exposed rafters with the plaster between them forming a series of concave curves. The rafters were painted white and the ceiling and walls a pale terracotta colour.

As Grey folded the doors back, an adjoining room was revealed. It also had two tall windows and now that she knew what to do, Lucia dealt with one while he did the other. Moments later the second room was filled with light, revealing it as an informal sitting room, the walls lined with books and pictures. Several large logs were visible behind the glass of a closed stove flanked by two comfortable-looking slip-covered sofas.

'This is delightful,' said Rosemary. 'For a minute I was beginning to wonder what we had let ourselves in for. Let's explore the bedrooms, shall we?'

'While you're doing that, I'll bring in the luggage,' said Grey.

The house had a bedroom and bathroom on the ground floor, and two more bedrooms sharing a bathroom upstairs.

'Grey had better have the downstairs room,' said his mother. 'We'll sleep up here. I'm used to a double bed, so I'll have this room.'

Lucia was pleased to be given the twin-bedded room because, while both rooms had two windows, hers were on different walls, giving different views of the surrounding mountains. She was looking at a framed collage of postcards from around the world, when she heard Grey coming up the stairs. After putting his mother's case in her room, he came along the landing with Lucia's suitcase.

Placing it on the bed nearest the door, he glanced round the room. 'I shouldn't care to have strangers in my house. Would you?'

'Perhaps they need the money they get from letting it,' she suggested.

'Perhaps, though the way it's appointed doesn't suggest any shortage of funds.' He tapped the antique tallboy near where he was standing.

'No, it doesn't,' she agreed. 'But perhaps they've had some reverses since they bought and furnished the house. Plans don't always work out. Things go wrong for people. Sharing your house with strangers must be better than having to sell it.'

'Maybe,' Grey said, with a shrug.

As he left the room, she thought how difficult it must be for a man who, all his life, had been cushioned by wealth, to understand what it felt like to be pinched for money.

The next day, while the two women were painting, Grey drove to the coast to see how much a small fishing port he remembered from his gap year had changed in the interval. It proved to be almost unrecognisable. Then scarcely more than a village, it was now a large and still-growing resort with new roads and roundabouts to accommodate the increased traffic.

But the small cove beyond the harbour was still much the same as it had been eighteen years ago. He spent an hour swimming and snorkeling before returning to the main seafront to have coffee in one of the many pavement cafés catering to tourists and to the elderly foreigners, obviously spending their retirement here, of whom he saw a large number.

On his way back to where he had parked the car, he noticed a bookshop, its window full of second-hand paperbacks, mostly with English titles. It crossed his mind that they might have a copy of a book his mother had been talking about at breakfast and Lucia had said she would like to read when they got back to England. He went inside and enquired.

Grey had gone to bed early, because he had bought a book he wanted to read in private, when there was a tap on his door. He closed the book and put it face down on the night table, taking another from the small stack before calling, 'Come in.'

His mother entered, wearing the blue cotton kimono he had brought back from a business trip to Japan.

'It's not like you to turn in so early, darling. Are you feeling off colour?' she asked.

He smiled at her. 'I'm feeling fine. I was up earlier than you were.'

He had gone out at first light and walked for an hour, following a track alongside the dry bed of the river. Large oleander bushes growing among the stones showed how rarely water flowed there.

Mrs Calderwood sat down on the end of the bed. 'It was nice of you to buy that book for Lucia. Are you feeling more kindly disposed towards her than you were at first?'

'You know I can't pass a bookshop. I happened to spot it when I was looking round.'

'That's dodging the question,' said his mother.

'Not so. I haven't examined my feelings about her. Men don't spend the hours in self-analysis that women do,' he said dryly. 'Not unless it's to do with something important such as business.'

'Human relationships are very important,' said Mrs Calderwood. 'If you weren't liking Lucia better than you did at first, I don't think you'd have bothered to buy the book for her. I don't see how anyone could fail to like her, once they get to know her.'

'I haven't spent as much time with her as you have. She seems a more acceptable person than I would have supposed a year ago,' he conceded.

'Sooner or later, I think you ought to have it out with her...why she did what she did. It would clear the air between you.'

'As far as I'm concerned all that matters is that she makes herself useful to you. As long as she serves that purpose, she won't have any problems with me. If she steps out of line, she will. It's as simple as that.'

Mrs Calderwood sighed. 'I suppose your attitude is natural. At least you aren't as rigidly unforgiving as your father and grandfather. They never transgressed themselves, and they both had draconian views on punishing people who did.' She wrinkled her forehead. 'What is the origin of that expression? I ought to know but I don't.'

'Draco laid down a legal system in ancient Athens. The punishment for almost everything was death,' said Grey. 'About a century later another statesman called Solon brought in a more lenient code and founded Athenian democracy.'

'How well-read you are! I'm a terrible ignoramus by comparison...but at least I understand people which I don't think you always do. "Judge not, that ye be not judged", my dear.'

She rose and moved closer to him, bending to kiss his forehead as she had when he was a small boy and she came in to tuck him up.

'It's lovely to have you here. You're such a joy to me, Grey. Goodnight. Sleep tight.'

'Goodnight, Mum.'

He watched her leave the room without looking back. There had been a catch in her voice when she said, 'You're such a joy to me.' He guessed that, when she didn't turn to smile from the doorway, it was because there were tears in her eyes.

She had always been easily moved but, for much of her life, had kept her feelings under wraps because his father had been embarrassed by emotion. Once, speculating on what their parents' sex life had been like, Jenny had remarked that it could never have been very satisfactory for their mother. He had agreed with her. But although he could discuss most things with Jenny, there was one thing he had never confided to her, a burden he could not share with anyone.

Closing his mind to it, he re-opened the book he had been starting before his mother's knock. It was the autobiography of a man who had spent his life imitating drawings and paintings by the old masters, and selling his work for large sums. He had done it so cleverly he had never been prosecuted. Grey hoped the book might help him to understand the mind of the woman in the bedroom above his own.

Lucia had heard the faint murmur of voices. Now, lying in bed with the book Grey had bought for her in her hands, she stopped taking in the words on the page and began to wonder how much, if at all, his kindness could be taken as indication that he was relenting towards her.

She could no longer pretend that his attitude was a matter of indifference to her. Slowly, reluctantly, she had come to realise that gaining his good opinion was increasingly important.

Perhaps all-important.

* * *

In her bedroom at the other end of the landing, Rosemary also had a book lying open on the turned-back sheet. It was a biography of her favourite cookery writer, but tonight it could not distract her from anxious thoughts about her son. She knew Grey wasn't happy and the only reason she could find was his failure, so far, to meet the right woman for him.

Apart from a wife and children, it seemed to her he had everything a man could wish for. He was at the top of his tree in the business world, had the means to maintain an enviable lifestyle and, although he had to work hard, he was able to take frequent breaks in the world's most exclusive holiday places.

Probably no one in his large circle of friends suspected that all was not well with him. But, being his mother, she knew there was something amiss.

Jenny, when Rosemary had broached the subject, had said, 'You're imagining it, Mum. Grey has it all, as they say. Most likely he has more and better sex than the average husband. His generation are chary of getting married…and being taken to the cleaners a few years later. If he had to split his assets, the amount his ex would walk away with would be in telephone numbers. And why would he want to have children when he has ours to amuse him…and can hand them back when he's bored with them?'

Remembering that conversation, Rosemary had to agree there was a lot of force in Jenny's observations. Today's world was utterly different from the time when she had been young.

'But everyone needs to be loved, Jenny,' she had reminded her daughter. 'That's a universal human need.'

'Women need to be loved. Most men would be happy to swop love for power, money and a new trophy wife whenever they're bored with the current model,' Jenny had replied. 'There are exceptions to the rule, but I don't think Grey is one of them. He's a realist, not a romantic.'

The exchange had left his mother depressed. She didn't want to believe that her adored son had everything but a heart.

At first, his arrival in Spain had made her wonder if he might be interested in Lucia. But tonight's brief chat with him had scotched that worrying idea. Rosemary liked the girl very much, and was glad she had been in a position to help her. But, élitest as it might sound to the younger generation, she felt it would be a disaster if Grey started taking a personal interest in Lucia. She had none of the qualities his future wife would need. She was from a different background. Above all, her fall from grace, though forgivable, would never be forgotten. For the rest of her life, there would always be someone raking up her past, reviving the gossip about her. That might not matter to a man who was not in the public eye, but it would be an embarrassment to anyone, like her son, whose activities did attract media attention.

Lucia was driving the hire car to the nearest small town in quest of fresh fish for supper when something shot out in front of her. She couldn't stamp on the brake because there was a red sports car close behind her. Feeling the impact as the creature was hit by her nearside front wheel, she flinched and switched on her indicator light, tapping the brake pedal hard enough to bring on the brake lights without reducing her speed significantly until the car behind had got the message that she was about to stop.

It was a straight stretch of road and she was aware

of the sports car pulling out and passing, but most of her mind was focussed on the casualty. As soon as the handbrake was on, she sprang out and ran back to see if the animal had been killed or severely injured.

It was a small grey cat. At first she thought it was dead. Then it opened its eyes and gave an agonised yowl, scrabbling with its front paws in a vain attempt to get up, despite badly injured back legs.

For a second or two Lucia froze with horror. She had no idea what to do. If she tried to lift it, it might claw her. There were no houses nearby. Where was a vet to be found?

The sound of running feet made her glance over her shoulder. The driver of the sports car was coming. Relief flooded through her, to be almost immediately replaced by fresh horror as she saw he was carrying a heavy metal implement.

He spoke to her in rapid Spanish. The only word she understood was *señorita.*

Scrabbling around in her memory, she dredged up a sentence she had learned by heart to explain her minimal command of the language.

Apparently guessing her nationality from her accent, the man said, 'Never mind, I speak English. Go back to your car, *señorita.* I will attend to this animal.'

'But you're going to kill it. Perhaps, if we took it to a vet, he could save it,' she protested.

The Spaniard looked doubtful. 'It may not be a domestic cat. Many kittens are dumped in the country by people who don't want them. They either starve or learn to fend for themselves. If they are injured, they can't hunt. I saw it run in front of your car. It may have been after a mouse.'

Wondering how he came to speak such idiomatic and

almost accentless English, Lucia said, 'In case it does belong to someone, I think we should try to save it.'

His shrug and the movement of his free hand was a gesture that, already, she recognised as quintessentially Spanish. 'Very well…if you insist. Wait here while I get some thick gloves. Even to bring a smile to those beautiful eyes, I will not risk having my hands torn to pieces.'

For an instant, his own almost black eyes held the teasing gleam of the incorrigible flirt. Then he ran back to his car, leaving her thankful for the luck that had brought him along this road at such an opportune moment.

CHAPTER NINE

HALF an hour later, when the cat had been admitted to the nearest veterinary clinic, Julian Hernandez, her rescuer, insisted on taking Lucia for a restorative cup of coffee in a nearby bar.

She welcomed the chance to have a proper conversation with a Spanish person. When, in answer to his questions, she had explained what she was doing in Spain, she asked, 'Do you live in this area?'

'No, no, in Barcelona. Have you been there?'

'This is my first time in Spain. I had a glimpse of Alicante as we passed it on the *autopista* on the way here from the airport.'

'Alicante is nice, but a small unsophisticated place compared with Barcelona. It's the finest city in Spain.'

'Better than Madrid?' she asked.

'Much better!' His dark eyes twinkled. 'I am a Catalan. For me Barcelona is the best city in the world.'

'What brings you down here?' she asked.

'The reason I speak such good English is because I had an English nanny when I was a little boy. She didn't marry until she was fifty-three when she met a man she had loved since she was sixteen. He had married someone else. By the time they met in Barcelona, his wife had died. They came to live on the coast here, the Costa Blanca as it's called. About ten years ago, Harry died and Nanny decided to move inland. She speaks fluent Spanish and preferred what she calls "real Spain" to the expatriate communities on the coast. But now she is over seventy and I'm trying to persuade her to come back to Barcelona where we can keep an eye on her in her old age.'

The expensive red sports car, his stainless steel and gold wristwatch and the quality of his clothes had already given Lucia the impression that he was well-heeled. What he had just said confirmed it.

A few years older than herself, but certainly not more than thirty, he was an engaging companion and by the time they shook hands—as even Spanish teenagers seemed to when greeting friends, she had noticed—she felt as if she had known him for far longer than a couple of hours.

During a salad lunch under the umbrella in the court-yard, she told the others about him.

'What a romantic story, but how sad that Harry didn't live to a ripe old age,' said Mrs Calderwood. 'Are you seeing this nice young man again?'

'He said he would keep me posted about the cat. Nanny, as he calls her, has a cat and she may be able to find out if anyone local has a pet that's gone miss-ing.'

'If the cat is badly injured, it would have been best to have it put down immediately,' said Grey. 'Animals aren't like people. They have no intellectual resources to make life bearable if they are badly disabled.'

'Did the vet suggest that, Lucia?' his mother asked.

'No, he said he would do what he could for it.'

'The vet has a vested interest in keeping the cat alive,' said Grey.

'What a cynical thing to say,' his mother protested. 'I'm sure no vet worth his salt would dream of letting an animal suffer unnecessarily. It's against everything they stand for.'

Her son lifted a sardonic eyebrow but made no further comment. Lucia wondered if he thought it was partly her fault the cat had been hurt. But even if he had been at the wheel, she doubted if he could have avoided hitting it.

A few moments later they heard the telephone ringing from inside the house.

'I'll get it,' he said.

Watching him spring up the steps to the upper terrace, Mrs Calderwood said, 'It may be one of the girls, ringing to ask how we are.'

But he didn't call her to the phone. A few minutes later he rejoined them. 'Mrs Alice Henderson wonders if you would like to join her for a drink at six thirty this evening. I said you were in the middle of lunch and would call her back.' As his mother was looking mystified, he went on, 'Mrs Henderson is the retired nanny Lucia's Spaniard is visiting. Probably the invitation was suggested by him as a way of pursuing their acquaintance.'

'I should think it's far more likely he thought Mrs Henderson would enjoy meeting your mother,' said Lucia. 'Even if she doesn't want to live surrounded by "expats", she may sometimes miss having a chat in her own language.'

'I should like to meet her,' said Rosemary. 'Where does she live, Grey?'

'In the next-but-one village along the valley. I wrote her address and the directions on the phone pad. You shouldn't have a problem finding it.'

'Aren't you going to come with us?'

'I think I'd be surplus to requirements. She wants to

chat to you, and I'm sure that Lucia's Spaniard would prefer to have her to himself,' he said, with a gleam of mockery.

Lucia found herself flushing. 'Julian is not *my* Spaniard,' she said, with emphasis. 'Actually he's a Catalan and clearly very proud of the distinction.'

'What is the distinction?' asked his mother.

Grey said, 'Catalonia is the most industrialised part of Spain. The Catalans are separatists. They regard the rest of the country as backward compared with themselves.' He rose from the table. 'Sit tight. I'll make the coffee.'

When he was out of earshot, his mother said, 'Grey seems rather fidgety. I think he suffers from withdrawal symptoms when he's away from the business for more than a few days. He's a workaholic, like his father. I wish he could learn to relax more. It's so lovely here, isn't it?'

'Yes, lovely,' Lucia agreed, watching the bees at work on a lavender bush.

But despite the peaceful atmosphere of the courtyard, she didn't feel very relaxed. Grey's repeated references to Julian as 'Lucia's Spaniard' had upset her. Grey seemed to be in a difficult mood, perhaps because, as his mother suggested, he was missing the cut and thrust of big business. But how could anyone hanker for that artificial world when they were here, in this much more appealing and real world? she wondered.

If he did, then his values were utterly different from hers.

Grey drove them to the meeting with Mrs Henderson. She lived in a terraced house with street parking along one side. The plastic blinds called *persianas* were down at all the windows facing the street.

Julian opened the front door, introducing himself to Mrs Calderwood and shaking hands before gesturing for her to pass down the dimly-lit hallway that opened out into a room further along. There, Mrs Henderson was waiting to greet them, but at first she could only be seen in silhouette against the light from the garden at the back of the house.

Lucia said, 'Hello, Julian,' and turned to introduce Grey. The two men shook hands.

It wasn't until they were all outside in the garden that she had a clear view of their hostess. She was not at all the cosy, somewhat infirm elderly lady she had visualised. Mrs Henderson's figure was spare, her thick iron-grey hair cut in a boyish crop and her tanned face as wrinkled as a raisin. She was wearing a man's shirt and trousers with sandals on her bare feet. She exuded energy and vitality.

Part of the garden was given over to an aviary occupied by various small birds. Near this was a staircase leading up to a flat roof.

'I'll lead the way,' said Mrs Henderson, and bounced up the stairs like a ten-year-old. 'I'm out most days, mountain-walking,' she said, as Mrs Calderwood joined her, followed by the others. 'I know all the old mule tracks for miles around. Julian is trying to persuade me to move to Barcelona but I should be like a caged lioness. I enjoyed city life when I was young, but not any more.'

While Julian was pouring out the drinks, Grey said to his hostess, 'I like your evil eye beads. Turkish, are they?'

'Ah, you recognised them.' Mrs Henderson's gnarled

hand went up to the necklace of bright blue beads, her only concession to femininity in her dress. 'Yes, I bought them from a market stall on a walking holiday in southern Turkey. Do you know that country?'

Grey said that he did and they had a conversation to which the others listened, Lucia thinking, not for the first time, how charming he could be when he chose. She wondered what it would be like to have the charm turned full-force on her. An unlikely eventuality.

About an hour later, Rosemary smilingly refused Julian's attempt to refill her glass. 'We must go. Thank you so much for inviting us, Mrs Henderson. The view from this terrace is lovely.'

'I am taking Lucia out to supper at a local restaurant,' said Julian. 'We'd be delighted if you would join us. Nanny and your son are obviously on the same wavelength,' he added, with a glance at the two now engrossed in a conversation about the western side of Spain.

'I think Lucia might prefer to have you to herself as you won't be here for long,' said Rosemary.

'I have decided to extend my stay,' said Julian, turning to look at Lucia.

The message was clear: he was interested in her. She couldn't help but be flattered. At the same time it was a complication she didn't want to have to deal with. She could see that, by any standards, he was an attractive man. But he didn't attract her.

There was only one man who did that. But there was no future in it. They would have to be shipwrecked on a desert island, with no hope of rescue, ever, before Grey would look at her the way Julian was looking at her.

'In that case, thank you, we'd be delighted,' said Rosemary.

When Grey found that his mother had agreed to eat out with Alice—as she had asked him to call her—and the smooth operator from Barcelona who persisted in calling her 'Nanny' in that asinine way, he was not pleased.

It was obvious to him that the guy was a womaniser who saw Lucia as a change from the glamorous, self-confident *señoritas* and bored-with-their-husbands *señoras* with whom he was accustomed to having it off. The fact that it would be difficult for him to set up the time to seduce her would add to the challenge. She would be no match for the Mediterranean looks, the bedroom eyes, the foreign accent; a combination that had been bowling over susceptible females since tourism had been invented.

The restaurant was only a short walk from the house. There was no traffic about and they walked in the roadway, five abreast, with the three women in the centre and the men at either end. Lucia was next to Julian who was telling her jokes and making her laugh.

Laughter transformed her, Grey noticed, making it possible to see what she must have been like at eighteen, before her father's illness, before her life had gone wrong.

But if she succumbed to Julian she would be making another error of judgment. Perhaps she was one of those women who had no judgment, who would go through life always making the wrong choices and fouling things up for herself.

CHAPTER TEN

FOR their date *à deux* the following night, Julian had booked a table at a restaurant overlooking the crescent-shaped Arenal beach at Jávea. The table was under the awning that, by day, shaded the terrace from the heat of the midday sun. On a balmy spring evening this was still the most popular part of the restaurant and the table reserved for them was one of the best, with an uninterrupted view of the sand and the sea.

Judging by the way he was greeted, Julian was a frequent and valued patron.

'What is that building at the far end, among the palm trees?' Lucia asked, when he had asked for *cava* to drink while they studied the menu.

'It's a *parador*...a hotel run by the State,' he told her. 'That one is modern, but many of them are in castles and other historic buildings. They're generally considered the best places to stay. Their charges are competitive and they serve regional cuisine.'

The *cava* turned out to be the Spanish version of champagne. It was accompanied by some appetisers in the form of stuffed olives, speckled quails' eggs and *huevos* de lumpo, the tiny glistening black eggs of the lumpfish, spread on pieces of toast.

When they had decided what to eat and Julian had chosen the wine, he leaned towards her and said, 'I don't understand your relationship with Grey. Explain it to me.'

'He's my employer's son.'

'But he doesn't approve of you having dinner with me. He scowled when I asked you last night. He glared at you when you accepted. I think he would prefer you to be dining with him.'

'No, no…you've got it wrong. He isn't interested in me in that way…only as a suitable travelling companion for his mother…which he doesn't think I am.'

'I know it is very difficult for artists to make a living, but I don't fully understand why you need to help her with her painting. Couldn't you find a more interesting job?' he asked.

'Perhaps, but this job was offered to me after I'd been out of the rat race for a while. My father was terminally ill and I gave up working to nurse him,' Lucia explained. At this stage of their acquaintance, she didn't feel it was necessary to tell him the other reason why she had been out of touch.

'I'm sorry to hear that.' Her right hand was toying with the stem of her wineglass and Julian reached out and put his hand on her wrist.

It seemed a spontaneous gesture of sympathy with no other implications. After pressing her wrist for a moment, he took his hand away. 'Is looking after Mrs Calderwood only a temporary expedient? Are you looking for something more ambitious?'

'Not yet. At the moment I'm enjoying the chance to see something of Spain. Long term I'm not sure what I want to do.'

But suddenly, as she spoke, she knew that it wasn't true. The ambitions she had started out with no longer inspired her. With her twenty-fifth birthday approaching, and thirty on the horizon, a new imperative was starting to seem important.

As a 'lonely only' herself, she had always visualised,

when the time came, having several children. All at once, in a flash of enlightenment, she knew that, if it were possible to arrange the future, she would choose to spend the next ten or fifteen years raising a family. Not only because she wanted children, but because as an artist she needed them. For some time, a secret pipe-dream had been to make a name for herself by writing and illustrating children's books. To do that, she needed to make a study of children, and where better than in her own family circle? But before you could have children, you had to find a man willing to father them. Any man wouldn't do. It had to be someone special. How ironic that, now she had found him, he turned out to be the last man in the world who would ever consider founding a family with her.

'You have a most expressive face,' said Julian, dragging her attention back to him. 'It reflects the nature of your thoughts in an intriguing way. In less than half a minute you have looked happy and excited and then very sad. What has been in your mind?'

'Oh…a dozen things,' she said lightly. 'You know how one's thoughts flit about from one thing to another. Tell me about your job, Julian.'

'I am the publicity and PR director for my family's boat-building business. It began, several generations ago, with a small firm building small fishing boats by traditional methods. Now we make yachts and motor cruisers to supply the demand from Spain's yuppies. All along this coast—' with a wave of his hand '—there are new marinas crowded with expensive pleasure craft, many of them made by us.'

'Do you enjoy your work?'

'There's nothing I would rather do. I wouldn't have wanted to be the boss, like my eldest brother, or the head of the accounts department, like one of my cousins. But the niche I have created for myself is most enjoyable. Before we paid a lot of money to agencies to promote our products and they didn't do a good job. I am doing a much better one,' he said, with a grin that saved his claim from sounding overly boastful.

Lucia contrived to keep him on this subject through most of the meal. She was genuinely interested, but also she wanted to avoid more questions about her life.

She didn't know the reason why Grey had been annoyed when Julian proposed tonight's date. She could only assume it was because he didn't approve of her enjoying herself. If he had his way, she felt sure, she would still be in prison and destined to remain there for some time.

'Now you are looking unhappy again,' said Julian, breaking the flow of his previous remarks. 'What have I said to remind you of something that troubles you?'

'Nothing,' she told him lightly. 'You're imagining it. Tell me more about your PR work.'

No 12 Calle Santa Josefina was in darkness when Julian stopped his car outside the front door and jumped out to open the nearside door for Lucia.

'Thank you, Julian. It's been a lovely evening,' she said, keeping her voice low, although all the bedrooms were on the courtyard side of the house and their occupants were unlikely to hear any but very loud sounds from the street.

'We must do it again,' he said, putting his hands on her shoulders and leaning forward to kiss her on both cheeks. 'Goodnight, sweet girl. Sleep tight, as Nanny used to tell me.'

She already had a key in her hand. He took it from

her, unlocked the door, pushed it open, then removed the key from the latch and handed it back to her. As she was re-locking the door, she heard him driving away.

The curtains at the hall windows had not been drawn and light from a street lamp attached to the front of the house gave sufficient illumination to make switching on the hall light unnecessary. Intending to make a cup of herb tea, she opened the kitchen door and immediately saw that one of the table lamps in the adjoining sitting room must have been left on.

She switched on the kitchen lights and walked round the corner, intending to turn it off. The room was not empty as she had expected. Grey was sitting on one of the sofas. There was a book in his hand and a tall glass on the end table beside him.

'Oh...I didn't think you'd still be up,' she said, disconcerted.

He put the book aside and rose, picking up the empty glass.

'I rarely go to bed before midnight. How was your evening out?'

'Most enjoyable, thank you. Did you and your mother go out?'

'Only as far as the village bar for a pre-dinner drink under the pepper tree.'

'I'm going to make a cup of tea. Would you like one?' she asked.

'No, thanks.'

He took his glass to the worktop and filled it from the flagon of spring water. 'Are you seeing Hernandez again?'

Something in his tone prompted Lucia to say, 'Possibly. Have you any objection to that?'

'Not as long as you realise that Spanish men tend to

regard women from northern Europe as more free and easy than their counterparts here. Don't be surprised if, next time, he sets up a situation where he can make a pass at you.'

'I should be *very* surprised,' she said indignantly. 'Julian doesn't strike me as a man whose approach to people is based on unreliable generalisations. I'm sure he would never overstep the bounds of friendship without clear encouragement.'

Grey put the glass to his lips and tilted his head to take a long draught of water. The movement drew her attention to the long strong column of his neck. She averted her eyes, annoyed with herself for registering a detail of his physical attraction at a moment when his mind-set was repugnant to her.

'He may take your going out with him as sufficient encouragement,' he said coolly. 'If you're not interested in him, why go out with him?'

'Because I *am* interested in him, but not in the way you mean. He's the first Spanish man I've met. Because he speaks perfect English means there's no language barrier between us. He's been telling me about his job...about Barcelona...about other parts of Spain. Have you never had any serious conversation with women? Are all your dinner dates set up with the objective you attribute to him?'

She had started out speaking calmly and reasonably. Then, suddenly, had lost patience with him and ended by snapping the questions in an openly hostile manner.

What happened then was as unexpected as a roll of thunder on a sunny afternoon.

In two strides he crossed the space between them, clamped his hands on her shoulders in a very different way from Julian's parting gesture, and leaned down to plant a rough hard kiss on her mouth.

CHAPTER ELEVEN

THE motive was so obviously punitive that she was almost as shocked as if he had struck her. And then, with a sound like a groan, he moved his hands outwards, over the ends of her shoulders and down her upper arms, before pulling her hard against him and continuing to kiss her but with rather more finesse.

Lucia was lost as soon as he touched her. She wanted to resist, to fend him off, to declare herself outraged and repelled. But she couldn't because, deep down, those reactions were not what she really felt.

Nothing she had read, or seen on a screen, or experienced, had prepared her for this overwhelming hurricane of profound life-changing sensations. All her normal controls evaporated. There was only one thought in her mind: that this was what she had been waiting for all her life; this man, this moment, this wildly passionate kiss.

When, finally, he let her go, the world had changed and would never be the same again. Trembling, breathless, dizzy, amazed, Lucia stayed where she was while Grey stepped back a pace.

'I didn't intend that to happen,' he said, his voice thick.

She could think of nothing to say. All she wanted was to be back in his arms, her mouth parted under his, her nerves like live wires transmitting erotic sensations to every part of her body.

'You said you wanted some tea,' he reminded her.

He moved away to where the electric kettle stood on a tray alongside lidded glass jars of coffee powder, Indian tea bags and herbal tea bags. After checking the water level, he took the kettle to the flagon and filled it.

Lucia was astonished he could function normally. She still felt like someone in shock. Surely it couldn't be his intention to behave as if nothing had happened?

'Grey...' she began huskily, what she wanted to say eluding her but knowing something must be said. They couldn't possibly go back to the way they had been before.

He plugged in the kettle, glanced at her over his shoulder. 'Yes?'

She braced herself. 'Why did you do it?'

Slowly, he turned to face her, placing the heels of his hands on the veined rose marble worktop behind him, his long fingers loosely hooked over the edge of it.

'I lost my temper...lost control. I'm not going to apologise for it. You're not a fool. You know how things stand between us. You challenged me. I reacted. It won't happen again.' He pushed himself away from the counter. 'Goodnight.' He walked out of the kitchen, closing the door quietly behind him.

Lucia heard the church clock strike one, two, three and four o'clock, with a single chime marking the half-hours. Probably people who lived here slept through the chimes undisturbed.

She wondered if Grey was asleep. Perhaps he had lain awake for a little while, annoyed with himself and even more annoyed with her for causing him to lose control. But she doubted if he were tossing and turning like she was. It would take something far more serious, such as a stock market crash, to keep him awake all night.

Buzzing around in her brain, like a wasp that refused to be waved away, was that enigmatic remark 'You know how things stand between us.'

What had he meant by it? How, seen from his perspective, *did* things stand between them?

She did not hear half past four strike and when she awoke the starry sky had been replaced by a blue one and the mountains were bathed in bright sunshine instead of being only dimly visible by moonlight.

To her dismay she discovered that, in the emotional confusion and shock of last night, she had neglected to set her alarm clock. It was now long past the time when they usually had breakfast.

Fifteen minutes later, after a quick shower to pull her together, she went downstairs to find Mrs Calderwood still at the breakfast table, reading a magazine.

'Good morning. I'm sorry I'm late down,' said Lucia.

'Good morning. It doesn't matter. Did you have a nice evening?'

'Yes, thank you, very nice.' Lucia wondered if Grey was round the corner in the sitting area, but did not look to see. She took an orange from the basket on the worktop and went to the sink to peel it.

'We'll be on our own from now on,' said Rosemary. 'Grey is on his way to the airport.'

Lucia swung round. 'He's gone?'

'He had an e-mail from London. Something important has come up. He needs to be there to deal with it. As he felt it would be a bore for us to run him to the airport, he organised a taxi.'

'I see…what a shame,' said Lucia. Had he told his mother the truth? she wondered. Or was the crisis at the office merely a pretext to remove himself from an embarrassing situation? Somehow, from what she knew of him, it didn't seem like him to chicken out of any situation, however awkward.

'Will he be coming back?'

'Probably not, he said. I think we've reassured him that we can cope on our own. Though it was lovely having him here. I expect you'll think me very silly and feeble, but I always feel more comfortable when there's a man around to deal with emergencies. Not, hopefully, that there will be any emergencies. But somehow I feel more at ease when Grey, or one of my sons-in-law, is on hand. Don't take that as a lack of confidence in you, my dear. That's not what I mean at all. It's an instinctive thing built-in with all, or most of, my generation...probably because the majority of us have never been as competent to manage our lives as your generation is.'

'You would never have made the hash of your life that I have,' said Lucia.

All the time she had been washing and dressing, she had been dreading confronting Grey again. But, in a curious way, his abrupt departure, for a reason she wasn't sure she believed, was even more upsetting.

Rosemary jumped up from the table and came to stand beside her, putting an arm round her shoulders. 'I thought you were starting to get over all that you've been through. You've looked so much better recently, Lucia. But this morning it's obvious you haven't had a good night. Did you have bad dreams...a nightmare?'

'I didn't sleep very well,' Lucia admitted. 'That's why I overslept. But please don't worry about me. Thanks to you I am getting over it. Even when it's your own fault, it's hard to come to terms with the fact that you can't ever wipe the slate really clean.' On impulse, she added, 'I think you believe how much I regret what I did, but I don't think Grey is convinced.'

'My dear child, what makes you think that? I know he didn't approve of this arrangement at first, but I'm sure he's changed his mind since then. What has he said to make you think otherwise?'

'Nothing explicit...but it's there in his manner. He doesn't trust me. He will never trust me.' Even as she spoke, Lucia knew it was probably a mistake to confide these feelings to his mother.

'I think, next time you see him, you should have it out with him,' said Rosemary. 'Grey is usually very direct himself, and he respects directness in others. My own feeling is that you've gone up in his estimation very significantly since that unfortunate scene on the day you arrived. You mustn't become over-sensitive, Lucia. If, at times, Grey has seemed distant or un-friendly, it's most likely because he has something to do with the business on his mind. Now: have your breakfast and let's plan our day. Shall we go to the market again and do some more sketching there?'

By way of the *autopista*, the run to the airport took a little over an hour. Grey passed the time chatting to the taxi-driver, partly to exercise his Spanish and partly to put off examining his reasons for fabricating an excuse to return to London when he would have preferred to stay in Spain.

Knowing that the charter flights from Alicante were subject to tedious delays, he had used his computer to book himself a first-class seat on a scheduled flight. But there was an hour to wait before it took off and, al-though the battery in his notebook was fully charged and he had the notes for a speech to knock into shape, he found it hard to concentrate.

The events of last night would not be dismissed from his thoughts. He could not rid himself of the memory of how Lucia had felt in his arms, how difficult it had been to stop kissing her.

He wondered what she had thought when she came down and found him gone. Her primary reaction had probably been relief. To have met at the breakfast table would have been embarrassing to them both. That she was physically drawn to him had been proved by her eager response. But it was her body, not her mind, that had betrayed her. How could she ever really warm to him when, effectively, it was his evidence that had put her behind bars?

That she had responded to him proved nothing except that she had recovered her natural vitality and, with it, the need for sexual fulfilment felt by any normal woman of her age. The irony was that while she obviously thought he indulged his appetite for sex on a regular basis, in fact this was not the case. For some time now he had found casual relationships increasingly unsatisfying. He wanted what his three sisters had; a stable relationship with a permanent partner. But first he had to find a way out of the impasse that was his present life. And there wasn't a way out.

The morning after Grey left, Julian rang up to ask if they would like to join him and Mrs Henderson on a picnic outing to a picturesque village further inland.

'He says it's tremendously paintable,' said Rosemary, who had taken his call and accepted the invitation.

The expedition proved to be most enjoyable. For an hour before lunch Rosemary and Lucia sketched a fine bronze moor's head fountain in the main square, while Alice pottered about, chatting to the locals in fluent Valenciano, the language spoken in the home. Julian took photographs with the latest thing in digital cameras.

After lunch, by a river that actually had a flow of water in it, Alice announced, 'I'm going to have a siesta for half an hour.'

'I think I'll join you,' said Rosemary. 'All that champagne is very sleepy-making'—with a smile at Julian, the provider of the *cava* and the picnic food.

'Lucia and I will stretch our legs along the river walk,' he said. 'You don't want to nap, do you, Lucia?'

She shook her head and, dusting crumbs from her cotton skirt, scrambled up from the rug, one of two he had spread on the ground for them.

On the opposite side of the stream at the centre of the riverbed a *pastor* was watching his mixed flock of sheep and goats grazing on the rough grass in a grove of almond trees.

'I wonder what he thinks about all day?' said Julian. 'I'd be bored out of my mind, wouldn't you?'

'I can think of worse forms of boredom.'

'Such as?'

'Oh…being stuck in an office typing all day,' she said. She couldn't tell him about the very worst boredom: being shut in a cell without enough books to fill the interminable hours.

Evidently this was not a topic Julian wished to pursue. He changed it by saying, 'So your watchdog has gone back to London, leaving you free to dine with me again tonight.'

'Thank you, but I can't leave Rosemary on her own.'

'She won't be alone. There's an English-language

movie showing at Calpe that will please both our old ladies. We'll drop them off and pick them up later. There's a good seafood restaurant down by the harbour. They can have supper beforehand. Better for their digestions.'

Lucia couldn't help laughing at the way he had everything planned. She wished she could feel as relaxed with Grey as she did with Julian.

Suddenly he seized her hands and swung her to face him. 'When you laugh like that I'm in danger of falling in love with you. But I think I had better not do that. My instinct tells me you like me, but only as a friend. Am I right?'

'Julian, we've only just met. How could we possibly be more than friends at this stage?'

'Many people go to bed with each other in less time than we've spent together,' he said, caressing her palms with his thumbs.

The sensuous touch had an effect on her, but not the one he intended. Immediately she remembered the sensations aroused by Grey the night before last.

She withdrew her hands. 'Please don't...let's keep it friendly.'

'OK...if you insist. Too bad I didn't meet you before he did. You're in love with him, aren't you?'

She thought of denying it, but suddenly the need to confide in someone was overwhelming. 'Yes...but I know it can never work out.'

'What makes you think that?'

'There are...reasons why Grey could never return my feelings. Insuperable reasons.'

'One of the maxims Nanny drummed into me as a small boy was ''Nothing is impossible if you really want to do it.'' It's true: very few things are insuperable.

What's the brick wall you think can't be climbed between you and him?'

'It's a long and complicated story that would probably put you off me too. I'd rather keep your good opinion.' But even as she said it, she knew she wanted to tell him. She needed to talk to someone and, once this trip was over, it was unlikely that her path and Julian's would cross again.

'Take a chance. Try me. Maybe I'll see a way to break down the wall that you've missed. At least I can give you a man's perspective on the situation, which is usually a whole lot different from a woman's.'

Lucia drew a deep breath. 'OK, I'll risk it. Three months ago I was in prison for fraud.'

As Julian's eyebrows shot up, she went on, 'Grey was one of the people I defrauded.'

As briefly as possible, she explained all the circumstances leading to her presence in Spain as Mrs Calderwood's painting companion.

'*Hombre!*' Julian was sufficiently astonished to revert to his native language.

'Now you can see why this particular barrier really *is* insuperable,' Lucia said, with a sigh.

For several minutes they walked in silence, Julian looking at the ground and chewing his upper lip, a mannerism she hadn't seen before and one that perhaps was reserved for situations he didn't quite know how to handle.

Finally he broke the silence by saying, 'If Grey is a just man, I think by now he will have realised that most people, if the pressure is strong enough, will do things outside their normal range of behaviour. You stifled your conscience because someone you loved needed expensive treatment that wasn't available unless you paid for it. What you did was totally out of character. If Grey really can't find it in his heart to forgive you, then I think you're better off without him. But have you talked to him about it?'

'There's no point,' she said. 'All the extenuating circumstances were emphasised by my defence lawyer. Grey wasn't in court when the lawyer made his appeal that I should be let off lightly, but I'm sure he read the newspaper report.'

'But he didn't know you then,' said Julian. 'Now he does. If I were you, I would have it out with him…ask him to forgive you. He'd have to be very hard-hearted to resist a direct appeal. For all you know, he may be waiting for you to approach him. What have you got to lose?'

It was Lucia's turn to bite her lip. Julian made it sound easy, but he was judging Grey's reaction by his own much more tolerant standards. The two men differed from each other in many ways. Grey was a harder, tougher, more commanding presence than the laid-back, easy-going Spaniard.

She said, 'Only my pride, I suppose—if he tells me he'll always despise me.'

'I don't think he will. If he despised you, he wouldn't have looked annoyed when I made a date with you.'

'Perhaps he was concerned that you didn't know the truth about me,' she suggested. 'Perhaps he was debating whether he ought to tell you.'

'I don't think it was *my* welfare he was thinking about. The vibes I was getting were more like the threatening signals made by the dominant male in a herd of animals when an outsider appears and looks lustfully at a pleasing young female,' Julian said, laughing. 'I think your misfortunes have depleted your confidence. You're extremely attractive. Do you think he doesn't see that?'

'You can be attracted to people without liking them,' she pointed out, remembering what had happened in the kitchen.

'True,' he conceded. 'But you're overlooking one important factor. Grey would never guess from your manner that you feel the way you do about him. He could be excused for thinking you were indifferent to him.'

'There have been occasions when I've shown that I liked him,' she said, turning her head away to hide the heightened colour that came when she remembered her unequivocal response to Grey's kiss. She hadn't made even a token resistance. He had touched her and all her defences had melted like snow in the sun.

'You may have thought so, but perhaps he didn't get the message. Next time you see him, try being really warm and open with him. Like you are with me. What is it about him that turns you on while all my best efforts to charm you leave you cold?'

'I don't know what it is about him,' she said thoughtfully. 'I think, when I saw him in court, I was impressed by him...even though it was mainly his evidence that led to my sentence.'

'Poor girl. I hate to think of you being shut up with real criminals. They should have put you in one of those open prisons you have in England.'

'I was a "real" criminal...with less excuse than some of the others whose backgrounds gave them no chance to become decent, law-abiding people. It opened my eyes to what awful lives some people have.'

He said briskly, 'I'm sure you don't want to talk about it, or even think about it. We had better be getting back or the old ducks may think we are lost.'

That night when, driving Alice Henderson's car, he dropped Rosemary and Lucia at No 12, he mentioned that in the morning he would be driving back to Barcelona.

'A charming young man, but an incorrigible flirt, so Alice tells me,' said Mrs Calderwood as they went indoors. 'His family want him to marry and settle down, but he prefers playing the field. No doubt Barcelona is teeming with beautiful girls.'

'I expect so,' Lucia said absently, thinking of Julian's advice and wondering if she would have the nerve to take it.

'Are you disappointed he isn't staying longer?' the older woman asked.

'No, not really. I liked him, but I wasn't smitten,' Lucia said lightly, wondering how Rosemary would react if she knew that it was her son to whom Lucia had lost her heart.

Several days passed pleasantly and uneventfully. When they painted in the village, people would come and look over their shoulders and pass incomprehensible remarks. Rosemary found this off-putting. Lucia had learned long ago to ignore it.

It seemed to her a huge waste that Rosemary's talent had gone unused for so many years. To her own generation, Rosemary's decision to turn her back on it was incomprehensible. Equally puzzling was the fact that any supposedly loving husband could have wanted his wife to neglect her gift.

Would Grey be like his father and insist that his wife concentrated on him and their children? Could I marry a man like that...even if I loved him? Lucia asked herself.

One lesson life had taught her, from observation rather than experience, was that people never changed their fundamental characteristics, though a lot of women believed they could change the men in their lives. She had never known or heard of anyone succeeding. She wasn't ever going to make that mistake herself.

Grey called his mother every evening, but not always at the same time. One evening he called early, when they were not long back from a painting expedition and Mrs Calderwood was in the shower.

Lucia picked up the phone. She knew that what Spanish people said to callers was *Digame*, but as the only people who rang them were Grey and Alice, she said, 'Hello?'

'Grey here. How are you?' From his tone no one would have guessed what had happened the night before his departure.

'We're both fine. Your mother is having a shower. Shall I ask her to call you back, or will you ring later?'

'I'll be out until past her bedtime. We'll talk tomorrow. What did you do today?'

'We went to an art gallery and then we pushed on to a village recommended by Alice. It has an old-fashioned wash-house still in use…mostly by little old ladies in black dunking their smalls but mainly having a gossip.'

The fact that he wasn't there in the room with her made it easier to sound relaxed, Lucia found. At the same time, talking to him by telephone made her more aware what an attractive and sexy voice he had. Its timbre activated some of the responses she had felt while locked in his arms.

'Sounds as if it might make a good genre painting,' he said.

She knew he meant the type of picture depicting a

domestic scene or an incident from everyday life. They were not in fashion at present, but she had always liked them. It sounded as if he did too.

'That's what we thought. We made a lot of sketch notes to work up when we get home.' She used the word 'home' without thinking. She wondered if it would annoy him.

'What are you doing tomorrow?'

'We're going to look at the castle and have lunch at a seafood restaurant.'

There was a slight pause before he said, 'Is Julian still around?'

'He's gone back to Barcelona.'

'Tell Mum I'll call her tomorrow. Goodnight... Lucia.'

Her answering goodnight was interrupted by the click as he cut the connection. But at least he had called his mother 'Mum'. Perhaps he saw the absurdity of being aloof when, if only for a few minutes, they had been on terms that made a nonsense of his previous formality.

Lucia replaced the receiver. It would have been encouraging to think that his enquiry about Julian had been prompted by something akin to jealousy. But she couldn't quite believe it.

She wished she had a recording of their conversation. She would have liked to play back 'Goodnight...Lucia', to play again and again the sound of his voice saying her name.

What would it be like to hear him say Lucia darling?

She was never likely to find out, but she couldn't stop herself wondering.

In his bedroom in London, Grey was tying a black silk bow tie with fingers made deft by long practice. He was going to a formal dinner after which he was going to speak. But as he had already memorised what he was going to say, and had long ago ceased to be nervous on such occasions, his mind was free to visualise the sitting room in Spain and the girl who, since his last night there, had been in his thoughts far too often.

Having kissed her, he knew it was going to be impossible to stop the situation there. The scent of her skin, the feel of her, would not leave him in peace.

Fixing platinum links left to him by his father into the cuffs of his dress shirt, he scowled at himself in the shield-shaped antique mirror on the top of the tall chest of drawers. You are being a fool, he thought angrily. Your life is complicated enough without adding another impasse to it. The other situation has no solution. This one you can at least try to resolve. Take her to bed and get her out of your system.

But, as he shrugged into his dinner jacket, he wasn't at all sure he could get Lucia into bed. Taken by surprise, she had not resisted being kissed, in fact had responded with unexpected enthusiasm. Bed, however, was something else. That she might strenuously resist, making an already uneasy relationship even harder to handle than it was at the moment.

It would have been better for them both if their paths had never crossed, he thought irritably. No satisfactory resolution was possible. But while it remained unresolved, the situation between them was a constant irritant. She was on his mind half the time…more than half. He was losing his greatest asset, his ability to concentrate on the matter in hand to the exclusion of everything else. *She* was becoming the matter in hand, by day, by night, all the time.

Raging, he left the room and, a few minutes later,

stepped on deck and made his way ashore to where a taxi was waiting to drive him to the hotel where the dinner was being held.

Three hours later, from the hospital, Lucia rang the number of Grey's mobile phone. She didn't get through to him and had to leave a message.

'Grey, this is Lucia. Your mother has been taken ill. I think she has had a slight stroke. They can't be sure until they've done some more tests. She's in hospital in Denia, being very well looked after. I've been advised to go back to the house now and come back here in the morning. The number to call at the hospital is—' She referred to the slip of paper she was holding, read it out and repeated it.

'I've also left a message on Jenny's answer-machine. Rosemary was most insistent that I shouldn't worry you, and I don't think you need be alarmed. But I felt you ought to know what was happening. Whatever time you get back, please don't hesitate to ring me.'

... not too worried sound. He was obviously anxious to throw a little extra weight around in the world before the airlines were too fully ...

Three short lines that the editors, fidgeting ...

CHAPTER TWELVE

IN THE taxi taking him home, Grey switched on his mobile and picked up four messages, the last being from Lucia.

She sounded as calmly in control as the sensible middle-aged woman who was his personal assistant and on whom he could rely to remain unflustered in all circumstances.

Yet he found that, while deeply concerned about his mother, he was equally worried about Lucia having to cope with a situation that must remind her of her father's illness and death. She wasn't ready to handle another crisis yet. She needed more time to recover from all she had been through before life dumped a fresh ordeal in her lap.

Leaning forward, he said to the driver, 'An emergency has come up. I need to get to Heathrow or Gatwick, or maybe even Stansted. It will take me ten minutes to change and pack. Can you drive me to whichever airport I can get a flight from?'

'Yeah, that's OK with me, mate.'

Grateful for modern technology that took most of the logistical hassle out of situations like this, Grey set about organising his unexpected return to Spain.

Lucia was not asleep when the telephone rang in the sitting room. She sprang out of bed and ran barefoot down the stairs. It might be Grey, or it might be the hospital. Wishing she had resisted their insistence that her presence there wasn't necessary, she prayed it was not the hospital.

'It's Grey. Did I wake you?' His voice sounded as close as if he were standing out of sight in the kitchen.

'No, I was still awake.'

'I'm on my way. I'm at Gatwick with a batch of charter passengers whose flight out has been delayed by the usual "technical trouble". Luckily there are a couple of seats to spare. We should be in Alicante by zero two hundred hours, local time. I'll check into a hotel and catch a few hours' sleep. Then I'll get a taxi to the village and we'll drive to Denia together. I'll be with you about half past eight.'

'Poor you...poor passengers,' she said, visualising the scene around him.

A planeload of weary people who had set out from home in a buoyant holiday mood that, after a long delay, had changed to exasperation. Probably there would be some exhausted, grizzling children among them. It would be a far cry from Grey's usual mode of travel in the pampered seclusion of first class.

'Yes, they're not a happy-looking bunch,' he said dryly. 'By the way, I've called the hospital and told them I'm coming. But I left strict instructions for them not to tell Mum. It might fuss her. Like a lot of her generation, she has a phobia about being a nuisance...would rather suffer in silence than cause even minor inconvenience to others. Crazy, but that's the way they are.'

'Your mother may protest when she sees you, but I have to admit that I'm very glad you're coming,' said Lucia. 'It's not that I can't cope. There are people at the hospital who speak excellent English. But when anyone is sick they need someone near and dear to them.'

Guessing how anxious he must be feeling, she added, 'According to some other foreigners who were in the hospital's waiting area, medical treatment in Spain is very good, even outside the big cities. I don't think you need to worry that she won't get the latest treatment for whatever the problem is.'

'I'll make sure of that,' he said. 'Get some sleep, Lucia. See you soon.'

As seemed to be his way, he rang off before she could reply.

For breakfast, Lucia peeled and chopped an orange into a bowl, added some cornflakes and topped them with a couple of dollops of *queso fresco*, the Spanish equivalent of fromage frais.

Taking the bowl and a mug of tea outside, she sat in the sun on the steps leading down to the courtyard. Despite a poor night's sleep, and her concern about Rosemary, she had the same sort of feeling she used to have on the day before her birthdays when she was a child. A sense of excited expectation.

She knew why: because Grey was coming. In an hour, or less, he would be here. They would be face to face for the first time since he had kissed her.

How wonderful it would be if she could greet him with the cheek kisses the Spanish exchanged whenever they met a relative or a close friend.

After he had rung off, she had gone back to bed and lain awake wondering why, when he had a bed here, he had chosen to stay in a hotel in Alicante for what remained of the night after his flight touched down.

The only explanation she had been able to think of

was that he thought it inappropriate for them to sleep under the same roof without someone else being present. It seemed a rather old-fashioned view for someone like him to hold, but perhaps it was in deference to his mother's attitudes.

Rosemary, though broad-minded in many ways, would almost certainly disapprove of two single people being in a house on their own overnight. More than once she had admitted to holding old-fashioned views on sexual relationships.

Perhaps, if she had lived with her fiancé for six months before their wedding, she would have realised he was a control freak and broken the engagement, thought Lucia. But would she necessarily have been happier with a less controlling man? Rosemary had loved her husband. He had given her every comfort. They had had four children, all of whom had turned out well. Maybe the loss of her chance to make a name for herself as an artist wasn't really such a high price to pay for a much better life than many people had.

Lucia was standing at the kitchen window when the taxi drew up outside and Grey emerged from the rear offside door. Seeing her, he raised his hand before bending to speak to the driver.

While he was paying the fare, she went to unlock the front door and open it for him.

The woman who lived in the house diagonally opposite, who had twice tapped on the window and presented them with a bag of freshly-picked lemons from the tree in her yard, was sweeping the path in front of her house.

'Hola…buenos días,' she called.

Lucia smiled and echoed her greeting, intensely conscious that in a moment or two she might be shaking hands with Grey.

But when she turned to look at him, he had a small grip in one hand and the case containing his notebook computer in the other. Clearly they were not about to 'press the flesh', as the saying went.

'Hello...are you exhausted? Was the flight a nightmare of unruly children and short-tempered parents?' she asked, stepping back for him to enter.

'The stewardess took pity on me. She found me a seat away from the main centres of bedlam,' said Grey.

She was probably hoping you would ask for her telephone number, thought Lucia. From what she had heard, debonair businessmen were in short supply on charter flights where most of the unattached men were likely to be the kind who spent their holidays sleeping off last night's hangover on the beach.

'Have you had breakfast?' she asked.

'Yes, but I'd like a cup of coffee before we leave. I'll just dump my kit in my room.'

The coffee was made when he reappeared. 'Shall we have it in the garden?' Lucia suggested, picking up the tray she had laid.

'Good idea.' As Grey took the tray from her, he gave her a searching look. 'How much sleep did you get?'

Did the question imply that she looked a wreck?

'More than you did, I expect,' she said, on her way to open the back door for him.

'According to last night's forecast, it will be pouring in London now,' said Grey when, having placed the tray on the garden table, he looked up at the sky where the only clouds were a few wispy mares' tails, indicating windy conditions at high altitude.

He sat down on the wooden bench. 'Now, fill me in on what happened.'

At the hospital, when they had been given permission to go to Mrs Calderwood's room, Lucia hung back.

'I'm sure your mother would like some private time with you. I'll go up and see her later.'

'Nonsense,' said Grey firmly. 'She'll want to see us both.' He took her arm and propelled her into the lift.

Rosemary was not in bed, but sitting in a chair by the window in her cornflower blue silk mannishly-cut dressing gown.

'Grey!' she exclaimed, her face lighting up at the sight of him.

He crossed the room to embrace her. 'I decided to take another break,' he said, as he straightened.

Rosemary looked suspiciously at Lucia. 'You didn't send for him, did you?'

'No, she didn't send for me,' said Grey. 'But she did, quite properly, leave a message to say what had happened and that you were in good hands. I should have been very angry with her if she hadn't. Anyway I was planning to come back.'

Presently, on the pretext of going to the loo, Lucia left them together and did not return for about a quarter of an hour. She found that they had been joined by a doctor she hadn't seen before, with whom Grey was having a conversation in Spanish.

She was introduced to the Spaniard and then the men resumed their conversation and Rosemary beckoned Lucia towards her and asked, 'Were you nervous, all by yourself at No 12 last night?'

'I might have been in an isolated country house, but not in a village house.'

Rosemary surprised her by saying, 'Tonight you'll have Grey there. In my day it would have raised eyebrows, a man and a woman alone in a house together. But nowadays anything goes. But if you're not comfortable with him being there without me, you have only to say so and he can find an hotel.'

'Unless he would rather stay close to the hospital, I'm quite happy about his being there,' said Lucia. 'As you say, lots of men and women share houses these days.'

'But usually not on a one-to-one basis, unless they're "partners",' said Rosemary. 'Anyway I'm hoping that tomorrow they'll let me come home. Today they're doing lots of tests. I'm beginning to feel a fraud. I feel perfectly well.'

Presently, after insisting they should not hang about but get out and enjoy the sun, she was taken away in a wheelchair to have the first of the tests.

'How do you think she is looking?' Grey asked, when his mother had been wheeled out of earshot.

Lucia thought it was best to be honest with him. 'Rosemary claims to be feeling fine, but I don't think she looks it. Do you?'

He shook his head. 'But hopefully this is the warning shot across the bows that will enable them to prevent something more serious happening later. Come on: let's do as she asks and find ourselves a sunny café.'

They spent the rest of the day to-ing and fro-ing between the hospital and various cafés in the surrounding town.

Late in the afternoon Mrs Calderwood said she was tired. Not having slept too well the night before, she was going to take a nap.

'I'll see you tomorrow, my dears,' she said, holding

out her arms to her son and then, after he had kissed her, to Lucia.

'Shall I drive?' said Lucia, when they reached the car park. 'You're beginning to look rather bushed. If you reclined your seat, you could have a nap on the way back.'

'I think I might do that,' he said, handing over the car keys.

They hadn't gone far before she saw that he was asleep, his head turned towards the window, showing the high slanting line of his cheekbone and the hard angle of his jaw. The fleeting glances she could spare from her attention to the road printed on her mind's eyes the shape of his eyelashes, neither straight not curly but something in between.

Careful to take bends slowly so that he wouldn't roll, and to avoid any bumps that might jolt him, she wondered what she could rustle up for his supper.

Grey was still soundly asleep when they arrived at No 12. She had to shake him awake with a hand on his shoulder.

He gave a murmur of protest, turning his head towards her, then slowly opening his eyes.

'Time to wake up. We're back,' she said quietly, seeing that it would take time for him to surface from the deep sleep induced by a broken night.

For some seconds his expression was puzzled as if he couldn't remember who she was. Then recognition came back and, with it, a sudden glitter akin, but not quite the same, to the fiery look in his eyes before he had kissed her.

Lucia drew in her breath, half expecting him to reach for her. But just then some local children went past. They were speaking Valenciano, a language less easy on the ear than Spanish. Their loud voices were a discordant intrusion. By the time they had passed, Grey was fully awake and unbuckling his seat belt. The electric moment was over.

After Lucia had unlocked the front door and they had entered the hall, he looked at his watch and said, 'Why don't we both catch an hour's sleep and then go out for supper?'

It seemed to her an excellent idea. By now she was beginning to droop. The thought of lying down and closing her eyes was alluring.

'OK...let's do that. Does your watch have an alarm?'

He nodded. 'I'll set it for seven-thirty, then have a shower and be ready to leave around eight...if that suits you?' he added.

'Perfectly. I'll see you later.'

She went upstairs, took off her shirt and skirt and fell into bed.

At one minute to eight she went down and found him opening a bottle of *rosado* from the fridge.

'An appetiser before we set out,' he said. 'Did you have a good sleep?'

'Marvellous. Did you?'

'Great. I like that dress.'

The compliment startled her, but she tried not to show it. 'Thank you.'

She concluded he had decided to be nicer to her, at least as long as his mother was in hospital.

He handed her a glass of the sunset-pink wine. 'Let's take our drinks outside. Any ideas about where we might go to eat?'

'There's a place at the top of the road on the other

side of the church. We could walk there. Then we don't have to worry about drinking and driving.'

'In that case you'd better take a wrap. It may be cooler later.'

It was during dinner, after her third glass of wine, that she said, 'Grey, I've never apologised to you for what I did. I would like you to know that I really am very sorry.'

He put down his knife and fork and leaned back in his chair, looking at her with an expression she could not interpret.

'You don't have to abase yourself, Lucia. You've already paid for what you did.'

'I thought you felt I'd got off pretty lightly.'

'I may have thought that at first. I didn't know you then. Now I think that, for someone like you, it was too harsh a sentence.'

'You do?' she said, in surprise.

Grey was still looking at her with that intent but inscrutable gaze. 'At the time of your trial I was too angry to consider the case dispassionately. I'd been made to look a fool...and you know how sensitive the male ego is,' he added, with the flicker of a smile.

'Some male egos,' she agreed. 'But I don't think you have an ego that needs to be constantly buttered. You were right to be angry. I behaved very badly. I'm ashamed of it now, but then...well, it's no use making excuses for myself. In my heart of hearts I always knew something was wrong, but I chose to close my mind to it.'

'Tell me about it,' he said. 'From what I know about you now, I'm sure that, before this happened, you never did a dishonest thing in your life.'

'I don't think I did…no. I was brought up to be honest. If I'd found a wallet in the street, I would have taken it to the police. I wouldn't have lied except to spare someone's feelings. But when it came to the crunch…when my honesty was tested…I failed.'

'Your defending counsel said you needed money for your father. At the time I thought that was a cooked-up sob story.'

'It was true,' she said, in a low voice. 'Dad's doctor admitted to me that the drugs he needed were available but they were very expensive. They could be prescribed in some parts of the country, but not in others…not in the place where we lived. The only way to obtain them was as a private patient. I thought it was worth a try, so I blocked out the suspicion that the pastiches I was painting were being passed off as originals.'

'In your place I'd have done the same,' said Grey. 'If I didn't have any money and my mother or sisters needed some expensive treatment, I'd rob a bank if I had to. Desperate circumstances lead to desperate measures. It's intolerable that you should have been placed in that position. The best available treatment should be available to everyone, no matter what it costs.'

'I could have mortgaged the house,' she said. 'But it would have been difficult to do without Dad knowing about it, and I knew he wouldn't agree. He was resigned to dying. He could be very obstinate. In the end, of course, he did die…so it was all for nothing.'

The waiter came back. *'Terminado?'* he asked.

The food had been served on the cold plates that seemed to be customary in Spain. Lucia had eaten her fish and courgettes but left the chips that appeared to be a standard accompaniment.

'Sí, gracias.'

Grey put his knife and fork together and indicated that he, too, had finished eating.

Before taking the plates away, the waiter recited a list of puddings which Grey translated for her.

'Pears in wine for me, please,' said Lucia.

When the waiter had gone, Grey refilled their glasses. Then he rested his left elbow on the edge of the table and put his hand in a characteristic position; his thumb under his chin, his forefinger up by his cheekbone and his second finger masking his upper lip. He appeared to be making a close study of the weave of the white linen tablecloth. She wondered what he was thinking.

Grey was thinking about Lucia's remark '…so it was all for nothing' and the proverb ''Tis an ill wind that blows nobody any good'.

Had it not been for her father's illness and what had followed, she would not be sitting here on the other side of the table, the candlelight emphasising the silky sheen of her hair, the bloom of sunshine and open air days on her skin, the soft fullness of her lips.

Her apology, obviously sincere, had crumbled the last of his resistance to her. He could no longer deny that he was within a hair's-breadth of being hopelessly in love with her.

But even if she had come to like him better than at the beginning of their acquaintance, he had no evidence that she felt more than liking. That she had responded to his kiss proved little beyond the fact that she was a warm-blooded woman who had had no man in her life for a long time.

Now circumstances had conspired to place them in a situation where it would be hard for him to control his desire for her. His common sense told him he must. His libido said, What the hell! Go for it! The two conflicting sides of his nature were in a precarious balance that could tip either way.

CHAPTER THIRTEEN

To Lucia, watching him but poised to look away if her scrutiny disturbed his train of thought, whatever it might be, he had never looked more attractive than by the softly-diffused light of the thick white wax candle burning inside a slightly tinted glass shade.

Not all Spanish people, she had discovered, had the dark brown eyes of the stereotypical Spaniard. That many did indicated how much interbreeding there had been with the Moors who had ruled much of Spain for many centuries. But everywhere there were Spaniards with eyes of other colours and Grey, with his dark hair and fast-tanning skin, could easily pass for a native of this country. Though many of the elderly people were noticeably short and often had the bandy legs that indicated poor nutrition when they were young, their children and grandchildren had grown up in happier times and were tall and well-built like Grey.

She was admiring his broad shoulders under the casual but perfectly-fitting cotton shirt he was wearing, when he looked up and caught her eye.

'Have you thought about the future yet? What you might do when you're ready to resume your career?'

Did the question imply that, despite what had seemed a détente in the cold war between them, he still wanted her out of Larchwood and his family circle?

'Not yet. As long as your mother finds me useful, I'm happy to stay. I'm not keen to go back to com-

139

mercial art, but that seems the only safe way to make a living.'

Her pears and his *flan* arrived. She had thought his choice would be a pastry or sponge cake filled with fruit, but it turned out to be what in England was called crème caramel.

'Good, I hoped it would be home-made,' said Grey. 'Sometimes they produce factory-made stuff in a plastic pot, but this is the real McCoy.'

Lucia's pears still had their stalks attached to them from which the thinly sliced fruit was arranged like a pair of fans.

'How would you feel about running an art gallery?' Grey asked her.

'I don't think I'm qualified...and who would employ me, with my history?' she added.

'Some people might consider your history a commercial asset,' he said, at his most sardonic. 'You are interested in pictures. You know a lot about them. The business side—book-keeping and so on—you could easily pick up.'

'Do you know of someone who is looking for a gallery-minder?'

'Not immediately, but possibly in the future.'

'I know beggars can't be choosers, but I really wouldn't want to work in London, or any big city. Larchwood has given me a taste for life in the country.'

'The gallery I'm thinking about—at present it's only on the drawing board and may not materialise—would be in a village or small town. If you were interested, I could put in a word for you.'

'Thank you, but at the moment I'm committed to working for your mother. If she didn't need me any more, then I'd have to look for something else. But I'm

hoping that tomorrow they'll tell her it was just a blip
that won't make a drastic difference to the way she
wants to live her life.'

'I hope so too,' he agreed. 'But it may be that, for
everyone's peace of mind, she will have to confine her
travels to the British Isles, or even closer to home.'

'Did the doctor advance any theories about what the
trouble might be?' Lucia asked.

'He thinks she may have had a transient ischaemic
attack. It's caused by minute fragments of blood or cho-
lesterol that clot in the brain and disperse of their own
accord. Or similar symptoms can be caused if the ver-
tebral arteries that run up the spine to the neck are ob-
structed, for example by looking upwards. Was she doing that before it happened?'

Lucia shook her head. 'Not that I remember.' After
a pause, she added, 'As Rosemary is slim and doesn't
smoke, I wouldn't have thought she was likely to have
high blood pressure.'

'Stress can cause hypertension. I think she was pretty
stressed while Dad was alive. He wasn't an easy man
to live with, especially as he got older. Perfectionists
seldom are.'

'Would you call yourself a perfectionist?'

He considered the question before answering it.
'Yes,' he said finally. 'But the difference between me
and Dad is that I'm not a control freak. I expect the
people who work for me to give one hundred per cent
of their energies to their jobs during working hours. But
outside the office I don't want to run anyone's
life…contrary to the impression you may have had
when we met at Larchwood,' he added dryly.

'Actually I admired you for being protective towards
your mother, even if—had you won the argument—it

would have deprived me of what you called "a cushy number".'

Remembering the circumstances in which he had made that remark—not during his first tirade in the drawing room, but looming over her while she lay in the bath—she found her colour rising.

Obviously Grey understood the reason for her discomfiture. 'Have you forgiven me for invading your privacy and catching you looking like a submerged Lorelei?' he asked, with a teasing gleam in his eyes that made her heart lurch.

Looking down at her plate to avoid that disturbing look, she said, 'I was angry with you at the time. Barging in like that seemed to demonstrate your utter contempt for me.'

'At the time that was what I felt. I was wrong. I'm sorry.'

Even without looking at him, she knew that he was sincere. When she did look up and meet his eyes, the expression in them made her unstable heart turn over. She had never expected Grey to look at her with such kindness that it could almost be taken for tenderness. Almost.

'Thank you…thank you for saying that,' she said in a low voice, trying not to show how deeply his words had moved her.

'Now that we've both apologised and reached a better understanding, our relationship should run more smoothly in future. Let's drink to that.'

He raised his glass, waiting for her to raise hers.

'And to your mother's return to good health,' said Lucia.

'To that also.' He touched the side of his glass lightly

against hers and they both drank some more wine, watching each other over the rims of their glasses.

The waiter came back. *'Café?'*

A timely interruption, thought Grey. 'Would you like coffee, Lucia?'

'Yes, please. *Café con leche* for me.'

For himself Grey ordered a *cortado*, a small cup of strong black coffee. He glanced around the restaurant, tonight not even half full, trying to distract himself from the image still in his mind of Lucia's beautiful body stretched out in the bath.

The memory of it was as clear as if it had happened yesterday. Vividly, in his mind's eye, he could still see her soft breasts, her navel, the tangle of curls concealing her Mount of Venus, the lines of her long smooth thighs. Her body had excited him then. It aroused him even more now that he knew what she was like as a person.

That was another matter they would have to address: what had happened on the last night of his previous visit. It could not be ignored, but how was he to explain that it could not be repeated, except on terms that she would find unacceptable and he was not happy about?

In the past his 'no strings' relationships with women hadn't bothered him. But that was then and this was now. Lucia wasn't a woman who, like the others, could use a man for her pleasure and, when it was over, forget about him.

If not totally innocent, she was certainly extremely vulnerable. The last thing he wanted was to embroil her in a relationship that had no future. The idea of causing her more pain was repugnant to him. Yet he wanted her. Wanted her powerfully and urgently.

* * *

The coffee came and, with it, a little dish of thin mint chocolates in dark brown paper sleeves. Lucia was intuitively aware that Grey still had something on his mind. He had seemed to turn his attention to the other diners but, as they were all members of the 'expat' retirement community who inhabited this part of Spain in large numbers, she couldn't believe he was really much interested in them.

In the light of their newly-established *rapprochement*, she decided to take a chance and ask him to clarify a remark that had been on her mind since the last time he was here.

'Grey, the night you kissed me, you said something about the way things stood between us. I wasn't sure what you meant.'

It seemed to her that, for a split second, he was startled by her frankness. She had surprised herself by bringing it into the open in such a calm, casual way.

'That's something I had intended to discuss with you,' he said. 'That you've raised it yourself makes it easier. What I meant, to be blunt about it, was that we're both aware of the attraction between us. It was inevitable, I suppose. We're single. We're neither of us in a relationship. We've been thrown together a good deal. Given those factors, it isn't surprising that we feel a mutual desire to go to bed together.' He paused, his grey eyes intent. 'Would you agree?'

Was he asking her to confirm that the desire was mutual, or that it wasn't surprising it should have arisen? Where was all this leading? Was he about to proposition her? To suggest that, given the freedom of his mother's absence, they should end the evening in his bed?

'I'd agree that you're a very attractive man and any

woman who spent time with you would be increasingly aware of it,' she said carefully. 'I know a lot of people think nothing of going to bed with other people simply because they fancy them. Personally, I don't think that's such a good idea. I think physical love should be kept for…important relationships.'

Grey drank some coffee. His hand was rock-steady, she noticed. Out of sight, on her lap, hers were trembling slightly. Even talking to him about making love played havoc with her normal controls.

'That's what I meant,' he said. 'But a serious relationship isn't possible for me at present. There are reasons why I want to stay out of…involvements. So I think it's best for us to ignore any feelings that go beyond friendship.'

'It was you, not I, who went beyond that boundary,' Lucia said coldly.

'With some provocation,' he reminded her. 'Don't be angry…or offended. I wish it could be otherwise, but unfortunately it can't. For us to become…involved could only lead to painful complications.'

Her pride came to her rescue. 'Aren't you being rather presumptuous in assuming that I would wish to become…involved?' she said, echoing his slight pause before settling for the word 'involved'.

She lifted her chin, an angry sparkle in her eyes. 'Because I didn't rebuff you when you kissed me isn't grounds for supposing that I would have been compliant if you had attempted to take it further.'

Suddenly the situation became untenable. She knew that she couldn't swallow another mouthful of coffee or pretend that nothing had happened while he called for and paid the bill. She had to get out of here.

'Would you excuse me?' She pushed back her chair,

picked up her bag and walked away from the table as if on her way to the ladies' room. Instead she walked past that door and out of the building.

She felt angry, hurt and humiliated. There could only be one reason why he was backing off from an emotional involvement with her: because he didn't consider her good enough to have any place in his life other than as a dogsbody to his mother.

How could she have been so stupidly mistaken as to think he was warming towards her...might even be starting to feel the way she felt about him? What a fool he must think her, to have to have it spelt out that she was beneath his touch and always would be.

She wondered how long it would be before he realised she wasn't in the cloakroom but had left the restaurant. By now she was halfway down the hill to the village. Suddenly it hit her that not only had she left her shawl on the back of her chair but she didn't have the key to the house. He did.

Biting back an expletive she had picked up in prison where most of the inmates used strong language as a matter of course, she regretted not bringing the spare key that hung on one of the coat hooks in the hall. To have to hang about in the street until Grey showed up was the last thing she wanted to do, but there seemed to be no alternative.

Had this been an English village, she could have gone to the pub and had another glass of wine. But she knew she would feel uncomfortable if she went into the bar here. At night it was a masculine stronghold. Even by day the local women didn't use it. They seemed to lead separate lives, sitting outside their front doors with their chairs turned away from the street as they gossiped with their neighbours, sometimes sewing or knitting.

Had the church been open, she could have sat in
there. But she was fairly sure that, except when a mass
was being held, it was kept locked.

She could go for a walk on the lanes that traversed
the small vineyards on the floor of the valley. But although it was bright moonlight now, there were clouds
spreading from the west and before long it might be
dark.

As Lucia was debating what to do, Grey was replacing
his billfold in his back trouser pocket and leaving the
restaurant, cursing himself for mishandling the situation.
A veteran of many delicate business negotiations, he
knew he had made a botch of something far more important to him.

At first, when Lucia had jumped up and left the table,
he had thought she was going to take refuge in the
washroom until her visible outrage was under control,
or had vented itself in a bout of angry tears in the privacy of a cubicle. Growing up with three sisters, he had
learnt early on that tears which, among men, were reserved for life's deepest griefs, were for women a more
frequently used safety-valve.

Despite that knowledge, the thought of Lucia in tears
gave him an uncomfortable feeling in his gut. Also, although the door to the ladies' loo was round a corner,
out of his line of sight, it had not been many minutes
before instinct had told him that she might have been
angry enough to walk out on him altogether. That she
had left her shawl behind was probably an oversight.

Questioned, the man behind the bar near the entrance
had confirmed that the *señorita* had left.

Now, as he strode down the hill in pursuit, Grey wondered what the hell he could say to put things right

between them...or as right as they could ever be while the present constraints on his life remained in place.

No acceptable explanation came to him. The real one he could not share with her. From her point of view, it probably wouldn't make sense. Women saw life from a different perspective. They had their own set of imperatives. A typical example of their thinking was his mother. She had given up everything else she valued out of love for his father. It had been a purely emotional decision made in the heat of a young girl's passion for a man unwilling to make any concessions.

It had been a mistake. But women were like that. The moment they fell in love, they threw common sense to the winds. She should have waited, tested the depths of her feelings. Instead, brought up to believe that there was only one true love in the world for her, and his father was Mr Right, she had jumped into a marriage that could be one of the reasons she was in hospital now.

His own experience was the opposite of hers. At nineteen he had suffered a bad bout of calf love that had served as a kind of inoculation and, for years afterwards, had seemed to make him immune, not to desire but to the tender feelings that made the difference between lust and love.

For some time he had tried to deny the tenderness Lucia evoked in him.

Now she had made it clear that although she found him physically attractive, she could never forget that he had been the instrument of her downfall, the man whose evidence had led to a nightmare ordeal that would probably give her bad dreams for the rest of her life.

'Aren't you being rather presumptuous...?' she had flung at him, and he could not deny it. On the strength of a single kiss, he had made a crass idiot of himself. He should have kept his mouth shut. What had he hoped to gain by half-explaining things to her?

Near the bottom of the hill, where the lane took a turn between two houses before joining a narrow street, Lucia looked over her shoulder. Having no serious expectation of seeing Grey coming after her, she was surprised to see him tearing down the slope, his long-legged stride covering the ground at a pace that meant when she reached No 12, he would probably have caught up with her.

Wondering what he would say, if he was in a black temper with her for walking out on him, she quickened her pace.

It had been light when they came through the narrow lane at the back of the church on the way out. Now, in the shadow of the granite-block building, it was dark. But even if Grey had not been following, she would not have felt any nervousness about who might be lurking in that dark space. The village felt a safe place.

I should like to live here, she thought. Then, unbidden, came the after-wish—with Grey. But she knew that was only a crazy pipe-dream. She could adapt to this simple rural life. Grey never could. His place in the world was fixed, and it was on a plane from which she was forever excluded.

There was no place for someone with a prison record in the rarefied atmosphere of his élite world.

He caught up with her moments after she reached the front door of No 12. Unfurling the shawl and holding it by its corners, he reached a long arm over her head and dropped it into place round her shoulders. It was done as swiftly and deftly as a matador swirling his cape.

'If I hadn't realised you had gone, you would have had a long chilly wait for me to come with the key,' he said dryly.

He sounded surprisingly calm. But she felt he must be furious inwardly. She was probably the only woman who had ever walked out on him.

Grey unlocked the door and reached inside to switch on the hall light. Then he stood back and gestured for her to precede him.

In the hall, Lucia said briskly, 'Goodnight,' and made for the staircase, fully expecting a hard hand to fall on her shoulder and spin her round to face him.

It didn't happen. He said, 'Goodnight,' and she heard him double-lock the door. Before she had reached the top of the stairs, he had gone into the kitchen, perhaps to make himself some more coffee.

She was still awake when the church clock struck one and then, a few minutes later, repeated the single chime.

By this time she was bitterly regretting the way she had handled things. Instead of making that stupid pride-driven remark about his presumptuousness, what she should have said was, What kind of painful complications?

Seconds earlier he had asked her not to be angry or offended. But, full of her own feelings, she had ignored that. Loving him, she should have been more sensitive to whatever was on his mind.

From downstairs came a sound that, had she been sleeping, she wouldn't have heard. The sound of a light being switched on at the far end of the hall. Moments later, straining her ears, she caught the sound of a door being opened and closed. Was he going to the bathroom next to his bedroom that doubled as a downstairs cloakroom when the owners of the house had visitors?

Mrs Calderwood sometimes went to the bathroom during the night but Lucia doubted if Grey did. In a few minutes she would know because, if only faintly, the flush would be audible.

When she didn't hear it, or the click of the switch as he returned to his room, she concluded that, like her, he couldn't sleep and had gone to the kitchen for a hot drink or possibly a nightcap.

This was confirmed when she scrambled out of bed and went to the window. A broad beam of light from the kitchen window was illuminating part of the courtyard.

In one reckless instant Lucia made a decision. Slipping her arms into the sleeves of her cotton robe, she pulled it round her and fastened the sash. Then, briefly, she used her hairbrush.

Barefoot, so that the sound of her mules on the treads would not announce her coming, she went down the stairs.

Taking a deep breath, she opened the kitchen door.

CHAPTER FOURTEEN

GREY was leaning against the worktop that divided the kitchen area from the dining space. There wouldn't have been room for a robe in the small grip he had brought with him. He was wearing a towel wrapped sarong-fashion round his hips.

Lit by downlighters fixed between the ceiling beams, his lightly tanned shoulders and chest had the sheen of polished stone. For a man in his middle thirties, he was in great shape, but his torso reminded her of sculptures of the Athenian athletes of Ancient Greece, not the ex-aggerated musculature of modern body-builders.

Straightening, he asked abruptly, 'What are you do-ing down here?'

'I couldn't sleep. I came down for a drink.' She glanced towards the electric kettle. It had a red light in the base that glowed when it was switched on. The light wasn't on at the moment.

'Water?' He opened the fridge and reached for a bot-tle of spring water stored on a shelf in the back of the door.

His movement revealed that behind him, on the work-top, was a tumbler of straw-coloured liquid that she took to be whisky and water.

'No, not water...a gin and tonic.'

She went to the tray where some bottles of spirits were kept. There were glasses in the cupboard above it. She took down a tall glass, removed the cap on the bottle of gin and poured out a generous slug. Gin and tonic had been her father's favourite drink. She had always preferred wine.

Behind her, she heard the snap and fizz of a can of tonic being opened. When she turned, he was holding it out for her.

'Thank you.' She took the can from him.

'Your feet will get cold...better drink it in bed,' he advised, making it clear he did not welcome her presence.

'Clay tiles aren't cold like terrazzo. I have more on than you do.' He was also barefoot, she had noticed.

His mouth compressed disapprovingly, but whatever he was thinking he kept to himself.

Lucia put her glass to her lips and swallowed some Dutch courage. 'As you're down here, shouldn't we talk?'

'It was you who cut short our last conversation,' he said curtly.

'I know, but—for your mother's sake—I'm prepared to go through the motions of being...friendly.'

He picked up his glass and drank from it. She had the intuitive feeling that, for reasons beyond her grasp, he was close to some personal snapping point. But he couldn't feel more tense than she did, poised to do something totally out of character. Or, if not out of character, certainly something she could only contemplate because she was desperately in love with him.

'Friendship is not an option,' he said dismissively. 'We can, as you say, put up a front for my mother's benefit. But we've both put our cards on the table and there's no viable meeting point. It's best if, as far as possible, we keep out of each other's way.'

'There is an alternative,' she said.

'If you mean your leaving—no. That won't do,' he

said flatly. 'It would worry and upset my mother. Anyway you're not ready to launch out on your own yet.'

'You underestimate me, Grey...I could survive on my own. But I don't think that's necessary. Life is about adapting to circumstances. Earlier tonight you talked about our mutual desire to go to bed together. Straight off the top of my head, as advertising people say, my reaction was guarded. Now I've had time to think it through. If neither of us wants a serious involvement, but we do want to make love together...then why not? Other people do...all the time. It's really not such a big deal.'

She moved towards him, put her glass on the counter and placed her palms lightly on his hard chest. Trembling inside, but outwardly calm, she tilted her face up to his. 'Let's go for it,' she said softly.

Grey's fingers snapped over her wrists like hand-cuffs. Knowing he didn't mean to hurt her, she managed not to wince.

'What's made you change your mind?' he demanded. 'At the restaurant you said you didn't agree with casual relationships.'

'You took me by surprise. Until tonight I've never been sure how you felt about me. I only knew how I felt about you.' She drew in her breath. 'I want you. I want you more than I've ever wanted anyone. I want to spend what's left of tonight in your arms.'

For an instant, before she closed her eyes and parted her lips, she saw the blaze of desire in the dark grey eyes looking down at her. The next moment she was in his arms, being kissed with a passion that wiped all thought from her mind, leaving her senses in charge.

The feel of his arms around her, the fierce ardour of

his kiss, was even more blissful than the kisses conjured up by her imagination. She relaxed into his embrace, swept away on a surging tide of emotion, not caring where it might carry her or where she might be washed up.

In the small part of his mind that was still functioning rationally as he crushed her pliant body against him and felt the intoxicating softness of her lips under his, Grey heard the warning bells and chose to ignore them.

He had been aroused from the moment she entered the kitchen, looking infinitely desirable in the thin robe that, when she moved, gave tantalising hints of the lovely body it concealed.

He couldn't believe she had offered herself to him so openly and generously. She had always seemed too reserved to speak with such candour. Her frank declaration of her desire for him had excited him more than anything any woman had ever said to him.

He kissed her until he could feel her heart hammering as wildly as his own. Then he picked her up in his arms and carried her to the door, using his elbow to depress the lever-type handle.

'I'll put out the lights,' she said, in a husky murmur, reaching for the switches.

In the seconds before the kitchen was plunged into darkness, he saw a glow in her eyes that had never been there before.

Neither of them had thought to draw the curtains at the windows in the hall and the light from the street lamp was enough to show him the way to his bedroom. It was Lucia who opened the door, and he closed it behind them with his shoulder.

As the room was not overlooked, he never drew the

curtains. The moon was no longer full, but still gave enough light to show the double bed and the rumpled sheet he had thrown off when restlessness had driven him to get up.

He set Lucia on her feet on the oriental rug between the end of the bed and the chest of drawers. Then he untied the sash round her waist and slid the robe off her shoulders. Her nightdress was made of some thin stuff that, in this light, was transparent. He could see the quintessentially feminine contours of her waist and hips and anticipate how silky smooth they would feel, in a moment, under his palms.

As the nightdress was not the kind that would slip off her shoulders and slide to the floor like the robe, he took handfuls of the filmy fabric and drew it upwards. She helped him by raising her arms like a child being undressed. Moments later she was naked.

For the second time he picked her up and held her against his chest, the feel of her cool bare skin and the first sight of her breasts making the blood race through his veins like a riptide.

He walked round the end of the bed and lowered her onto the mattress, letting her go reluctantly for the moment it took him to shed the towel round his hips.

When he undid the towel, and dropped it, and Lucia saw the whole of his tall strong body in all its magnificent masculinity, there was a small fraction of time when she wondered if she was mad to have offered herself to him without the smallest degree of commitment on his side; on the contrary, a plain and unequivocal disclamation of commitment.

Then she knew that it didn't matter. She loved him as she would never love any other man. If this one night was all she would ever have of him, it would be better than nothing: one brilliant memory to treasure for the rest of her life.

Love was about giving, and her body was all she had to give him.

She lifted her arms to embrace him. A moment later he was beside her, sliding his arms beneath her, bending his head to kiss her.

The sun was shining when she woke up, alone.

A small clock on top of the chest of drawers showed it was nearly eight. She had overslept by an hour. Not surprising, considering how little sleep they had had.

A song came into her head. 'One Night of Love'. She had heard it on the radio while she was nursing her father, in a programme on hit songs of the past. Sung as a duet by a man and a woman with the perfect articulation fashionable in the days of wind-up gramophones and records three times the size of compact discs, it had stayed in her memory, not the words but the title and the lilting romantic tune. She hummed it now as she lay wondering where Grey was.

Perhaps in the bathroom next door. Or perhaps making coffee in the kitchen. Was he feeling as good as she was? How many times had they made love? She hadn't kept count. She only knew that every part of her, from her ears to her insteps, had been kissed and caressed in a way it would have been very easy to mistake for the real thing.

The way she had made love to him *had* been the real thing. But she doubted if he would guess it. He would think she had more experience than was actually the case, never suspecting that it was her love for him, not lots of practice, that had made it easy to toss away all inhibitions and do whatever came naturally. Things she had only read about, never done with anyone else.

Now, in the bright light of morning, it made her blush a little to remember everything she had done in the silvery shadows of the night.

Presently, coming down to earth and remembering that they had to go to the hospital, she jumped out of bed, retrieved her nightdress and robe from the back of the chair where he must have put them this morning and, without pausing to put them on, hurried out of the bedroom to go to the upstairs bathroom for a quick shower.

Had Grey opened the kitchen door while she was passing it, it wouldn't have bothered her. The passion they had shared in the small hours had taken her far beyond the sort of embarrassment she might have felt at being caught naked by him yesterday.

It took her twenty-five minutes to brush her teeth, shower, dry, put on clean clothes and attend to her hair and make-up. She was on the landing, about to go down, when she heard voices in the street. Two people, a man and a woman, were conversing in Spanish. Even though he wasn't speaking his own language, she recognised the man as Grey.

Lucia opened the nearest of the landing's windows and leaned out. Below her was their Spanish neighbour, wearing her quilted dressing gown—a garment that in rural Spain was acceptable street wear—and waving her hands in the air. Smiling down at her, holding the drawstring bread-bag that usually hung behind the kitchen door, Grey was looking happier and more relaxed than at any time since Lucia had known him.

'*Buenos días,*' she called down to them.

They both looked up. She saw Grey's smile fade,

changing into an expression she could not define. Then he made some polite excuse to their neighbour and moved towards the front door.

He was closing it behind him as Lucia walked down the staircase.

'Good morning,' she said again. 'You've been to the baker's, I gather. I didn't think you knew where it was.'

'I didn't. I asked,' he said, walking into the kitchen and putting the bag on the worktop.

And then, as she joined him, he took her in his arms and kissed her.

Presently he said, 'I thought you'd still be asleep. I was going to bring you breakfast in bed.'

'Let's have it in the garden,' she suggested, knowing that what she would rather do was forget about breakfast and go back to bed.

In the moment before he withdrew his arms from around her and turned away to start fixing the coffee, it was evident that Grey had the same idea. But also that he wasn't going to act on it.

Lucia put out a tray and the necessary china and cutlery. While she busied herself, she wondered if Grey intended to talk about the change in their relationship or if, from a man's point of view, there was nothing to discuss. It had happened and that was that.

The first thing he said, when they were sitting at the garden table, now spread with a checked gingham cloth, was, 'Whether or not Mum is allowed to leave hospital today, I think they'll advise against her flying home. I'm going to call Larchwood and tell Jackson to bring the car down. It won't take him long to get here using the French autoroutes.'

'Does he speak any French?'

'No, but he'll manage. He's a resourceful guy. It'll be an adventure for him.'

Lucia peeled a mandarin to eat with the freshly-baked *barra* Grey had wrapped in a napkin to retain its warmth. When he opened the napkin and offered her the basket, the fragrant aroma seemed to encapsulate the magic of this place where, if only for a little while, she had experienced unforgettable happiness.

'Perhaps I'll ask Braddy to come with him,' said Grey. 'She was a nurse for a short time before she married. She's the ideal person to look after Mum on the way back. That would leave you free to fly back with me...via Paris. We could spend a few nights there and be back by the time they arrive. How does that sound to you?'

'It sounds wonderful...but what is your mother going to think about it?'

'At this stage, she doesn't have to know. It's better she isn't aware of any...complications until she's fully recovered. She'll think we're going straight back to the UK. Three is a crowd in the back of the car and for you to sit beside Jackson wouldn't please him. He likes to have the front to himself.'

'It still seems rather...deceitful,' said Lucia. 'And what if something went wrong and they needed us...especially you?'

'If there were the smallest likelihood of that I'd arrange for her to be taken home in an ambulance. We have insurance cover for that contingency. Otherwise Jackson can keep in close touch with me by mobile. He can call me without knowing where I am.'

He drank some coffee, watching her closely over the rim of the cup. The look in his eyes was the one she had seen from the landing window but failed to interpret.

His tone was matter-of-fact as he went on, 'The crux of the situation is that you and I need some time together. Apart from the pleasure aspect, there are things I need to tell you…discuss with you.'

'Can't you tell me now?'

'There isn't time.' He looked at his watch. 'By the time we've finished breakfast we'll need to leave for the hospital.'

It wasn't clear to Lucia why they couldn't discuss whatever it was on the way there. But she didn't intend to press him. The longer she knew him, the more strongly she sensed that Grey was a man already burdened by pressures she could only guess at. She didn't intend to add to them. If he wanted to postpone the discussion, so be it. Love was about giving people whatever they needed. If he needed her to be patient, she would do her best to contain her own urgent need to know where they were heading…if anywhere.

On the way to the coast he didn't say much. But, on a straight and quiet stretch of road, suddenly he took one of her hands from her lap and kissed her knuckles.

'Did my beard rasp your lovely skin last night?' he asked. 'I should have taken time to shave. But one doesn't think of those things in the heat of the moment.'

'I didn't notice,' she said, smiling at him. It wasn't strictly true. She had been dimly aware of the roughness of his cheeks and chin, but it had been a part of his maleness; one of the many exciting differences between them, like the muscular feel of his backside and the hard power of his shoulders.

Now, as she watched his hands on the steering wheel, she longed to feel them caressing her. It made her feel guilty, but she couldn't help hoping the medics would want to keep Mrs Calderwood in hospital for another twenty-four hours.

Then she and Grey could spend another night together, which wouldn't be possible with his mother in the house. It wouldn't feel right to make love with Rosemary in the room above them. Lucia had an uneasy feeling that, despite the older woman's extraordinary kindness to her, she would not be pleased if she knew what had happened last night.

At the hospital, Grey parked the car. As he pulled on the handbrake, he turned to her. 'This may be our last time alone for a while. Let's make the most of it.'

He released his seat belt and, leaning closer, took her face in his hands and kissed her.

Lucia fumbled to release her own strap and, when it was free, and regardless of who might be looking, slid her arms round his neck, returning the kiss with enthusiasm. For the first time in her life, she understood the overwhelming need for another person that drove people to do mad, reckless things.

It was Grey who broke off the kiss. 'We must stop this before...' His voice husky with desire, he left the sentence unfinished.

As they drew apart, he gave her a rueful grin. 'You'd better go in ahead of me. I need to cool down for a minute.'

The admission pleased her. If only she could have the same effect on his heart.

'OK.' She touched his cheek. This morning it was closely shaved, but still the texture of his skin was different and subtly exciting.

She got out of the car and made her way to the hospital's entrance.

CHAPTER FIFTEEN

SHE found Mrs Calderwood out of bed and dressed.

'Where's Grey?' asked his mother, after they had exchanged good mornings.

'He'll be here in a minute,' said Lucia. 'Did you have a good night?'

'Not bad, but tonight I'll be back in my own bed...I mean the one at No 12,' said Rosemary. 'They're letting me go, thank goodness.'

'That's wonderful,' said Lucia, firmly quashing her own secret disappointment that she would have to wait until Paris to spend another night in Grey's arms.

'They've been very kind to me, but it's a peculiar feeling...being in a hospital where you don't speak the language,' said Rosemary. 'It makes you feel like a child...not in control of the situation. What's keeping Grey? Is he talking to one of the doctors?'

'I think that was his intention when he sent me ahead,' said Lucia, feeling this answer was allowable as there was no way she could tell his mother the true reason he was delayed.

'I expect from now on he'll try to wrap me in cotton wool,' said Rosemary. 'It wouldn't surprise me if he tries to put an end to these trips of ours, but I'm not going to stand for that. In high summer it's too hot and crowded to travel unless you have to go then, like parents of school-age children. But in September I thought we might go to the Greek islands.'

Grey caught the tail of this remark as he joined them.

'That depends on your health, Mum,' he said, crossing the room to kiss her.

'I'm sure my health will be fine. I refuse to be mollycoddled.'

When, on the drive back to No 12, she learned that Grey had already instructed Braddy and Jackson to set out for Spain as soon as they could, Rosemary was indignant.

'That's ridiculous, Grey. A completely unnecessary expense.'

'I don't think so, and nor does your doctor. I had a taste of charter flying when I came down here this time. For someone who hasn't been well, it's far too stressful. You'll enjoy a leisurely run back through France. Lucia and I will fly back.'

To Lucia's surprise, his mother did not question this arrangement, though she continued to grumble about his fussing.

That night they all turned in early. But although she had a lot of sleep to catch up, for some time after switching off her light Lucia lay thinking about Grey in the bedroom on the ground floor.

She felt sure there was no possibility of his tapping softly on her door, nor did she wish it to happen, with his mother in the next room. But she was counting the days until they would be alone again.

What was he going to tell her when they reached Paris? Was he going to invite her to become his mistress until such time as he tired of her? But such an arrangement wasn't practical while she was working for his mother. Perhaps he was going to suggest that she transferred to his payroll.

Would he really have the gall to suggest that she

become, in effect, his toy? Did he think that, because she had once closed her eyes to the possibility that her work was being used for illicit purposes, there was nothing she wouldn't stoop to?

Thinking about it, she reached the disturbing conclusion that, where Grey was concerned, she had no moral scruples. If he wanted her, he could have her...on any terms. After all, who would be hurt by her becoming his mistress? Only herself. She had no parents to be ashamed of her. No close friends at hand to deplore her behaviour.

Then another aspect of the situation struck her, making her give a stifled groan. There were his mother's feelings to be considered. She would disapprove strongly of her son and her protégée being linked in an irregular relationship. Like most of her generation, Mrs Calderwood accepted but did not concur with people living together, and certainly not when there was no intention of permanance. The idea of Grey having a mistress would be anathema to her.

I couldn't hurt her like that when she's been so good to me, thought Lucia wretchedly. A couple of nights in Paris that she will never know about: that I can't deny myself. But anything more...no, it's not on.

Two sleepless nights in succession, for different reasons, left Lucia looking decidedly wan the next morning.

Last night Grey had insisted that his mother have breakfast in bed. When Lucia went down to the kitchen, the kettle was switched on but the bread-bag was missing from the back of the door. She began laying a tray for his mother, tensing a little when she heard the front door opening. Would he seize the opportunity to kiss her? Or did he intend to stay at arm's length until they arrived in Paris?

She did not have to wait long to have her question answered.

He came into the kitchen, tossed the bag on the counter and put his arms round her, the way he had yesterday morning.

'I missed you last night. Did you miss me?'

'Yes,' she admitted.

'Good.' He bent his head and kissed her the way he had in the car, with the same effect on them both. 'I want you. It's hard to be patient,' he murmured, close to her ear.

Lucia drew back. 'You mother might disobey your orders,' she pointed out. 'I'm sure you don't want her to walk in and find us like this.'

'Not at the moment—no,' he agreed. 'But it's very hard to keep my distance.'

Nevertheless he moved away from her, leaving her feeling curiously bereft. Being in his arms felt so right, so natural.

It was Lucia who took Mrs Calderwood's breakfast tray up to her. She found Rosemary propped on all four of the double bed's pillows, gazing out of the window at the mountains across the valley.

'"Look thy last on all things lovely, Every hour",' she quoted. 'Who wrote that?'

'I think it was Walter de la Mare,' said Lucia.

'Until something happens to remind us, it's so easy to forget that life doesn't go on for ever,' said Rosemary.

'I know. I took freedom for granted until I lost it,' said Lucia, placing the tray across her employer's lap. She straightened and looked at the mountains. 'I wonder, if we lived here, if we'd feel trapped after a while. It seems a paradise now, but—' She left the sentence unfinished.

Part of the reason the valley seemed like paradise was because Grey was here. Without his presence, it would still be a beautiful place but her heart would be somewhere else...wherever he was. Conversely, places where she wouldn't choose to go—arctic wastes, deserts, jungles—would be endurable if he was there.

'I like to travel, but I should never want to live abroad,' said Rosemary. 'I should miss the girls and my grandchildren. I like to be close to my family.'

It was on the tip of Lucia's tongue to say, But what if your family wanted to go to the ends of the earth? Would you make them feel they were deserting you? She kept the thought to herself. Fortunately none of Rosemary's brood had been footloose. But Lucia's father, when young, had given up the offer of a job on an Australian newspaper because it would have upset his mother to part from her only son.

There was a tap on the door and Grey came in.

'I've just had a call from Braddy. They crossed the Channel by the Euro Tunnel yesterday afternoon, found a comfortable place to spend the night and had a first-class dinner. By tonight they'll be close to the border. Once they're over the mountains, it won't take them long to get here. They might make it by tomorrow night.'

'Where can they stay?' said his mother. 'They'll need a rest before we set out for home. I must say, nice as it is here, I am rather longing to be back in my own surroundings.'

Grey said, 'There's a small *hostal* near the next village, catering mainly for mountain-walkers, so the baker tells me. I'll go and see what it's like. Would you like to come with me, Lucia? Mum will be OK on her own for the short time it will take us to check the place out.'

'Yes, do go, my dear,' said Rosemary. 'You know the sort of place Braddy will or won't like. I don't want her to come all this way and be uncomfortable when she gets here. Jackson won't care what it's like as long as it's clean. Men don't mind having to rough it, but Braddy is a bit of a fusspot.'

To be alone with Grey, even if not for long, was an unexpected bonus. However on the outward drive he kept their conversation on impersonal matters and Lucia did not feel encouraged to raise the subject in the forefront of her mind.

The *hostal* was a bit on the spartan side, but the showers and loos were immaculate and they both felt that Braddy would find it acceptable for the short time she would be there.

All the way back to No 12, Grey talked about Jackson who, thirty years earlier, had once been another of his mother's 'lame ducks'. They had met in court, she on the magistrates' bench and he, then in his twenties, on a charge of being drunk and disorderly.

'She offered him a job as a handyman. If my father had known, he would have been as furious as I was when she brought you to Larchwood,' said Grey, with a sideways glance. 'Her judgment was sounder than ours. Jackson has more than justified her faith in him, and so have you.'

'I haven't been around long enough to prove that,' Lucia said lightly.

'You've proved it to me.' His tone and his smile were warming beyond measure.

But, later, during lunch, his mother said something

that quenched Lucia's optimism that, despite all the signs against it, they might have a future together.

Following a remark by Mrs Calderwood about how lucky she was to enjoy the support of two such 'faithful retainers' as Braddy and Jackson—she had waggled her forefingers as she used the archaic expression—Lucia said, 'Do you think they might marry? They seem to get on very well.'

'Oh, no, I'm sure that won't happen,' said Rosemary. 'In some ways it would be rather convenient. They could share the cottage, leaving me an extra bedroom for when we're a "full house" at Christmas. Jackson might like the idea. I've often suspected he has a soft spot for Braddy. She likes him, too...but only on a friendly basis. They're from entirely different backgrounds. He grew up in what's nowadays called a dysfunctional family. Braddy's parents were very nice people.'

'Does that matter now they're both middle-aged?' said Grey.

'It matters at any age,' said his mother. 'Marriage isn't an easy relationship, even for older and supposedly wiser people. Any kind of imbalance must make it even more difficult.'

Lucia's heart sank. If Rosemary thought Braddy and Jackson getting together would be a hopeless *mésalliance*, she would be appalled by Lucia's wishful thinking. Clearly the gulf between herself and Grey would be seen by his mother as an unbridgeable abyss. Perhaps it was. Perhaps that was why he was looking displeased, because he didn't want to be reminded that—from his mother's perspective—by making love to Lucia he was behaving in a way she would consider unprincipled.

* * *

Grey was displeased by his mother's lack of tact. He knew the construction Lucia would put on the remark about imbalance. Although she was good at hiding her reactions, instinct told him she had been hurt.

There were times when, though he loved his mother dearly, her outlook and attitudes stretched his patience to breaking point. Perhaps when he was her age, he would cling to the manners and mores of the past, but he hoped not.

When they had finished lunch, he would have liked to take Lucia out for a walk and explain the whole situation to her. But it was neither the time nor the place for that. It was better to wait until they reached Paris where he could break it to her gently, taking it a step at a time, testing the ground as he went. That she loved him, he was in little doubt. But whether she loved him enough…that was a question only she could answer.

alone in a bedroom with male or the possibility of any-
 body looking in on their privacy, Lucia felt extremely shy
and awed by the situation, looking at Lui especially
in the...

CHAPTER SIXTEEN

MRS CALDERWOOD and her party set out on their leisurely journey after breakfast. They were taking the
road north, Grey and Lucia were driving south. Before
they left, Grey gave the keys to No 12 to Amparo, the
neighbour who kept an eye on the place in its owners'
absence.

When he came back and got in the car beside Lucia,
he said, 'Alone at last!'

The grin that accompanied this remark made her own
spirits lift. Since her farewell embrace with his mother,
she had been feeling guilty about the furtive nature of
her trip with him. Not being frank and open about it
made it seem like what her father would have called a
dirty weekend.

By lunchtime they were in Paris, being driven to their
hotel. It was not, to Lucia's relief, a dauntingly grand
establishment, but quite a small place in a side street.
Perhaps the kind of hotel where men took women whom
they didn't want to be seen with in public, was her next
deflating thought.

The bedroom allocated to them—they were given the
key and left to find their own way to it—was at the
back of the building, overlooking a small but attractive
garden with sunbrella-shaded tables where a couple
were having a drink. It looked a pleasant place to relax
after a long day of sight-seeing.

Although it was only a few nights ago that they had
been locked in each other's arms, now that they were

alone in a bedroom with little or no possibility of anyone intruding on their privacy, Lucia felt curiously shy.

She stood by the window, looking at but not really taking in the details of the surrounding buildings, trying to think of something to say.

It was Grey who broke the silence. Sounding wholly at ease—but for all she knew he might have been in this situation many times before—he said, 'I'm going to ask them to send up a bottle of wine. Would you like a shower before we go out for lunch?'

'Yes...yes, I would,' she said eagerly.

'Go ahead.' He sat on the side of the bed and picked up the telephone. As she had already discovered in the taxi and at the reception desk, his command of French was as fluent as his Spanish.

He was still on the telephone when, having unpacked her toilet bag and her robe, she disappeared into the bathroom. It had a shower compartment, handbasin, bidet and loo. Talking about their night stops in France, Braddy had complained about the inadequate size and thin pile of French hotel bath towels. But the ones here were large and fluffy.

Lucia undressed and hung her clothes on the pegs on the back of the door. She had washed her hair and blow-dried it before going to bed last night. As she didn't want to get her hair wet, she used the shower cap provided, with other giveaways, by the management.

The warm water relaxed her. It had been stupid to be tense, she told herself. Whatever Grey was going to tell her couldn't alter the essential fact that she loved him. Today, this hour, this moment, being the only time that anyone could be sure of, it made sense to relish the present and not think about tomorrow.

At which point the bathroom door opened and she

saw Grey's tall figure as a blurred but recognisable shape through the patterned glass walls of the shower cabinet. The next thing she registered was that he had no clothes on. A moment later he opened the door and stepped in beside her.

'May I join you?' he asked, smiling down at her.

'Why ask when you've already done it?' said Lucia, somewhat abruptly.

The reason she was less than welcoming was the shower cap. She knew she looked horrible in it. What woman didn't? Even the expensive frilly kind of cap did nothing for anyone, not even a beautiful girl, which she was not.

'Why are you cross?' asked Grey, putting his arms round her to draw her close to him 'Because I didn't kiss you the moment we were alone? I wanted to, believe me. But I used to hear my sisters complaining about guys who pounce too soon. My problem—' he paused to touch her lips lightly with his '—is that, the moment I kiss you, I want to make love to you, no holds barred.'

He kissed her again, more lingeringly, caressing her back with his hands.

Lucia closed her eyes and forgot the unbecoming shower cap.

Several hours later they left the hotel and stepped into the legendary street life of one of the world's most romantic cities.

'It's a little late for lunch, so let's have a *croque-monsieur* to stave off the pangs until dinner,' said Grey, taking her hand in his. 'Does that sound OK to you?'

'It sounds perfect...even though I don't know what a *croque-monsieur* is,' said Lucia smiling.

'A toasted sandwich, generally cheese and ham. But there may be something else we'll like better when we see the menu.'

Although it was a few degrees cooler than it had been in Spain, the weather in Paris was warm and the pavement cafés were full of people chatting, or reading, or watching the passersby.

They found a café that wasn't too crowded. A waiter brought them a menu and Grey ordered coffee to drink while they made their decisions about what to eat.

When that had been done, and the coffee brought, he said, 'I can't put it off any longer. This is the moment of truth…when I put my cards on the table and you read my fortune.'

Lucia wasn't sure what he meant by that, but decided to hold her tongue and let him explain in his own time without asking questions.

'Most of my adult life I've been living a lie,' he said, his grey eyes suddenly sombre. 'For various reasons, I've pretended to be someone I'm not…and have no wish to be. Like a lot of bad habits, it started when I was at university. Up to that point I hadn't given any serious thought to the rest of my life. My parents had always assumed I would follow my father into the family business and I'd gone along with that because there was nothing more attractive in view.'

Their waiter reappeared with a little basket of quails' eggs, a larger basket of crusty bread and two pots of butter.

'*Bon appetit, m'sieur…'dame.*'

While they were peeling the thin speckled shells from their first eggs, Grey said, 'Then I began to realise there were other kinds of lives than the one my family and most of their friends lived. Not everyone was obsessed by business and golf, like my father and the men he mixed with. There were other options.'

As he buttered a piece of bread, not for the first time Lucia felt the urge to draw the strong masculine hands whose touch could be firm or gentle.

'To cut a long story short, I knew that I wanted to break out from the mould made by my grandfather,' Grey went on. 'But I wasn't sure what I *did* want to do. Without being able to present my father with a positive alternative to his plans for me, there wasn't much point in resisting the pressure to conform. Perhaps what I should have done is walked out and made my own way in the world. But that would have caused a good deal of distress. Am I making any sense to you?'

'Of course,' said Lucia. She told him about her father's sacrifice of his plans. 'I think not wanting to wound their parents has influenced a lot of people's lives.'

'Probably,' Grey agreed. 'The forces that shape people's lives are very strange and complex. I always knew I wanted to travel, but I didn't have a specific reason for travelling. Now I do—but also an equally strong reason why it may not be possible.'

He paused to drink some coffee before saying, 'It wasn't until my late twenties that I found what the French call a *raison d'être*…a reason for existence. I began to be seriously interested in paintings. Learning about them, visiting the world's great art galleries whenever I had the chance, filled one of the voids in my life. Eventually that interest led to my second *raison d'être*—you, my sweet girl.'

Startled, she swallowed a crumb the wrong way and had to gulp down some coffee to avert an inelegant coughing fit.

'Me?' she said huskily, when she could draw breath.

'You,' he said gravely. 'And I don't think you would be here if you didn't feel warmly about me. But the problem is this: I am not who you think I am. I want to cut loose and run from the past...and the present. I want to begin a new life. But it's not the kind of life most women want to share.'

She was still knocked sideways by what he had said moments earlier. 'What is it you want to do?' she asked, to give herself time to recover her self-possession.

'First, I want to chuck the business...to have no further part in the running of the company. That will horrify my mother and it won't delight my sisters. Julia is expecting me to keep the CEO's seat warm for her eldest son who appears to be keen on the idea. Even if she lives into her nineties, as I hope she will, Mum will always have a comfortable income. But the rest of the family are less secure and won't be happy if their Calderwood incomes plummet, as they may after I resign.'

'I don't think they can expect you to go on doing something that bores you in order to make *their* lives more comfortable,' said Lucia. 'What do you want to do instead?'

'I want to set up a gallery, not in London, somewhere in the country. But I don't want to run it myself. I want to travel the world, learning more about other cultures' art and buying pictures to re-sell. I should also like to create a showcase for it on the Internet. The few friends I've discussed this with think I'm out of my mind. Perhaps you do too?'

'I think it's a great idea, and I'd love to help you with it...if you'd like me to? This is the same gallery you were talking about the night we had dinner isn't it?'

'Yes, but at that time we weren't on the same terms that we are now. I would want you to help me, but not as the gallery's minder. I would like you to travel with me…as my wife,' he added quietly. 'I'm in love with you, Lucia. I would like you to be part of my new life. But I know it's asking a great deal…asking you to sacrifice everything that women need and want.'

'Like what?' she asked, puzzled.

'Women are nesters by nature. They need somewhere settled and safe.'

'You're generalising,' she said. 'Women aren't all alike.' Her mouth twisted. 'How many women have been in prison? Hardly any.' She leaned towards him and drew a deep breath. 'I need only one thing, Grey. For you to love me as much as I love you.'

He reached for her hands. 'Darling, you think that now, but a lifetime is a long time. It won't always be Paris on a warm summer evening…we won't always want to go to bed as urgently as we do today. You need to think this over before committing yourself.'

'I'm already committed. I have been for ages. I just didn't see how you could possibly lose your heart to someone so wildly unsuitable. Don't say I'm not because we both know I am.'

'Unsuitable for the man I've been trying to be, perhaps. Not for real Grey Calderwood. You don't actually know him yet.'

'I've caught glimpses.' She reached out to touch his cheek with her fingertips. 'Isn't marriage always a voyage of discovery? Neither of us is going to be the same person in ten, or twenty, or thirty years' time. But if we grow and change together, the chances are we'll feel the same way about each other when we're your mother's age as we do now.'

'I would certainly hope so,' he said. 'But she is one of the reasons why I'm concerned that you shouldn't let yourself be blinded by emotion…as Mum was.'

'I wonder if she was? Or if, deep down, she knew that she didn't have what it takes to be an important artist? I know I don't have that inspired vision of the world. Perhaps Rosemary knew it too. Perhaps marrying your father made it easier for her to come to terms with it. It's quite hard to admit to yourself that you won't ever be in the front rank.'

'That's one of the things I love about you,' he said, 'that you're gentle with other people's feelings. You would never hurt her by letting her know that you know her talent is only a small one. The only person whose feelings you haven't handled with kid gloves is me, and I guess I was fairly brutal to you at first.'

'You were horrible,' she told him, laughing. 'But I have to admit you were entitled to be. I will try very hard to make amends. When are you going to break all this to your family?'

'As soon as George has given Mum a check and advised me on whether the shock of my resignation would be bad for her just now. Our news we'll tell her at once. That's something that can't be put on hold. The only way I can endure being a square peg in a round hole for a little longer is if my evenings and nights are spent with you.'

Presently they left the café and strolled in the direction of the Seine, recapping their whole relationship and explaining why they had behaved as they had, both misleading the other into thinking they were in a no-win situation.

On one of the wide tree-lined *quais* between the many bridges spanning the river, Grey said, 'The last time I came down here I was by myself. There was a girl leaning against that tree, with a guy kissing her. They made me wonder how much longer I was going to live on my own. It's an unnatural existence, being single. Men and women were designed to live in pairs, don't you think?'

'I couldn't agree more,' said Lucia, as he steered her towards the tree, put his arms around her and his hands on the trunk, and kissed her.

'Hugging a tree takes on a whole new meaning when you do it like this,' he murmured against her mouth.

Not caring who might be watching—Paris had that effect on her—Lucia put her arms round him.

'It's hard to imagine you feeling lonely. You always seem so self-sufficient,' she murmured, leaning into him, his chest being a more comfortable support than the trunk of a tree.

'I hope I am…up to a point,' he said, resting his chin on the top of her head and moving his hands from the tree to her waist. 'People who have no inner resources can be a burden to everyone. On the rare occasions when my father couldn't go to the office or play golf, he drove everyone crazy. He didn't read, he didn't listen to music, he never walked except on a golf course. When I was old enough to analyse myself and my family, I realised that any woman with my mother's looks and social skills would have satisfied him. I sometimes wished I was like him in that way.'

He put his hand on her chin and tilted her face up to his. 'But I needed somebody special. I had almost given up hope of ever finding you. When you did turn up, it wasn't love at first sight. Do you realise that, if you hadn't defied me that first day, if you'd taken my cheque and done what I wanted—got lost—our paths would have diverged, never to cross again? Now, I can't bear to think of you out there, alone in the world, with no one to love and protect you.'

Later they had dinner at Le Thoumieux, in the seventh *arrondissement* not far from the Eiffel Tower. It was, so Grey told her, a classic turn-of-the-nineteenth-century bistro, with banquette seats, walls lined with huge mirrors, gilt chandeliers and waiters wearing huge white aprons.

The speciality of the house was duck, either *confit de canard,* the preserved duck, or the *cassoulet,* a traditional white bean, sausage and duck stew.

'If we have the stew, we'd better pass on a starter. It was created to satisfy hard-working country people's appetites,' said Grey.

'In spite of the quails' eggs, I feel amazingly hungry,' said Lucia. 'Maybe it's making love that has whipped up my appetite.' After their walk, they had returned to the hotel and spent another hour of delirious pleasure in bed.

'Don't worry: sex uses up lots of calories,' said Grey, the amusement in his eyes betraying that he was teasing her. 'Anyway you can afford to put on a pound or two. Curvy women are much more attractive than the twig insects in the fashion magazines.'

The delight of being on these easy, bantering terms with him was a joy it would take her some time to get used to. But even though she was now very close to perfect happiness, the thought of his family's reactions was a cloud in the sky that could be ignored for the time being but was not going to go away. She could only hope there wasn't a storm brewing up which, even if it could not destroy their love, could leave a trail of bad feelings and bitter reproaches in its wake.

CHAPTER SEVENTEEN

FOR her wedding outfit, Lucia chose a slim-fitting plain white crêpe dress with long sleeves, a skirt that stopped just short of her ankles and a neckline that skimmed her collarbones. With it she was going to wear the single string of matched cultured pearls presented to her by Braddy.

'I'd like you to have them, my dear,' the housekeeper had told her. 'I haven't any daughters or nieces to leave them to, and my own neck has collapsed. It would please me to see them shown off to advantage on your pretty young neck.'

Mrs Calderwood had wanted the service to be held in her parish church and the reception at Larchwood. Despite having organised three weddings for her daughters, she had claimed to be disappointed when Grey insisted on a quiet civil marriage and a reception limited to family and very close friends at a hotel in London, before he and Lucia flew off to honeymoon at a secret destination.

Whether her future mother-in-law was genuinely disappointed and was putting a brave face on the situation, Lucia could not tell. It was also hard to be sure what Grey's sisters thought. Like their mother, the two elder daughters were women who would feel it was not good manners to let their reservations be seen. If Grey was set on the marriage, they would accept it gracefully, whatever they might feel privately.

The worst shock for them had been his announcement

of his resignation from the board. That had been a blow to them all, and all four of them had come to her privately and begged her to persuade him to reconsider. She did not think they had believed her when she'd said, 'Grey's happiness is the most important thing to me...and I think he's old enough, and wise enough to know what is best for him.'

To that reply, Jenny, more blunt than the others, had said, 'I think he's mad. If he walks out, the company will fall apart...the way they invariably do when the driving force vanishes. I admire you for being willing to go along with this dotty idea of his, but I think you'll both regret it.'

'The one thing I *did* regret, I don't any more,' Lucia had told her. 'Those awful months in prison were a small price to pay for the rest of my life with Grey.'

She was remembering that conversation as she picked up the wide-brimmed hat of fine white straw, trimmed with moiré silk ribbon tied in a large crisply stiff bow at the front, that completed her outfit.

As she placed it carefully on her head, Lucia wondered if Jenny was right and Grey's plan would turn out, in retrospect, to have been a dotty idea. As far as she was concerned, it didn't matter. It was what he wanted to do, and her idea of marriage was an alliance in which both partners did their best to let each other have whatever they wanted—dotty or otherwise.

In any case, she had total confidence that, if Plan A didn't work out to his satisfaction, Grey would swiftly come up with Plan B. He was the kind of man with whom she would always feel safe no matter what contingencies and vicissitudes might be lying in wait for them.

Disregarding many of the traditional wedding conventions, they had planned the occasion to suit themselves. They had spent the night apart, Grey on the boat, Lucia at the hotel where, last night, he had given a party for some of his friends who had not been invited to the reception.

The bedside telephone rang. Lucia picked up the receiver. 'Hello?'

'Mr Calderwood is in the lobby, Ms Graham,' said a voice.

'Please tell him I'll be down in a moment.'

There was nobody else in the lift that took her down to the lobby. She hoped Grey wasn't expecting a full skirt and a filmy veil. She had tried on a selection of outfits and this was the one that had felt right.

When the lift doors opened, he had his back to her. He was taking a turn round the lobby. He was wearing a light grey suit she hadn't seen before, the impeccable tailoring enhancing the natural breadth of his shoulders and the straightness of his broad back. Whenever she looked at him now, no matter how formally he was dressed, she had an X-ray type vision of the strong male body under the uniform of the urbane businessman. Not that he would be wearing that uniform for much longer. From now on he could dress as he pleased.

As she stepped out of the lift, he turned, saw her, and came striding towards her in the eager way that always made her heart lurch. She still couldn't quite believe this man, who could have had anyone, wanted her.

'It's all right: I'm not going to knock your hat sideways or smudge your lipstick. I know better than that,' he said, taking her hands and lifting them to his lips.

He was wearing a pale yellow silk tie. A yellow carnation was tucked in his buttonhole.

'I missed you last night,' he told her. 'For the next

fifty years, let's try to spend as few nights apart as possible.'

'Sounds good to me...but maybe this hat was a bad choice if it's putting you off kissing me properly.'

'A careful kiss then.'

He ducked his head to avoid the brim and kissed her lightly on the cheek and even more lightly on her mouth.

Straightening, he said, 'You look ravishing.'

When he looked at her like that, she felt ravishing. She wondered why she had ever thought his eyes cold, his expression hard.

'There's a taxi waiting. Let's go, shall we?' He clicked his heels together and offered her his forearm.

She took it, feeling the sinewy strength of bone and muscle under the expensive cloth.

She still didn't know where they were spending tonight, but she didn't need to. Anywhere Grey chose to take her would be fine with her. She wasn't about to surrender her independence of thought or her capacity to make some decisions on her own. She would still sign her paintings Lucia Graham. She would always be her own person, but still bound heart and soul to Grey.

He put her into the taxi and climbed in behind her. As the vehicle moved off, he reached for her hand and they laced their fingers together.

The last minute nervousness Lucia had expected to feel had not materialised. She realised she was no longer worried about what her future in-laws might think. Suddenly full of confidence, she relaxed and enjoyed what she knew would always count as one of the happiest moments of her life, being a bride on her way to her wedding.

An emotional new trilogy by
bestselling author

Rebecca Winters

Three dedicated bachelors meet thrills and danger
when they each fall captive to an innocent baby—
and clash mightily with three exciting women
who conquer thier restless hearts!

Look out for:

THE BILLIONAIRE AND THE BABY
(HR #3632) in December 2000

HIS VERY OWN BABY
(HR #3635) in January 2001

THE BABY DISCOVERY
(HR #3639) in February 2001

Available in December, January and February
wherever Harlequin books are sold.

Harlequin Romance®

Experience the ultimate desert fantasy with this thrilling new Sheikh miniseries!

Four best-loved Harlequin Romance® authors bring you strong, proud Arabian men, exotic eastern settings and plenty of tender passion under the hot desert sun....

Look out for:

His Desert Rose by Liz Fielding
(#3618) in August 2000

To Marry a Sheikh by Day Leclaire
(#3623) in October 2000

The Sheikh's Bride by Sophie Weston
(#3630) in November 2000

The Sheikh's Reward by Lucy Gordon
(#3634) in December 2000

Available in August, September, October and November wherever Harlequin Books are sold.

HARLEQUIN®
Makes any time special.™

Visit us at www.eHarlequin.com

HRSHEIK2

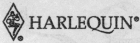
HARLEQUIN®

makes any time special—online...

eHARLEQUIN.com

your romantic life

━Romance 101━
♥ Guides to romance, dating and flirting.

━Dr. Romance━
♥ Get romance advice and tips from our expert, Dr. Romance.

━Recipes for Romance━
♥ How to plan romantic meals for you and your sweetie.

━Daily Love Dose━
♥ Tips on how to keep the romance alive every day.

━Tales from the Heart━
♥ Discuss romantic dilemmas with other members in our Tales from the Heart message board.

Tyler Brides

It happened one weekend...

Quinn and Molly Spencer are delighted to accept three
bookings for their newly opened B&B, Breakfast Inn Bed,
located in America's favorite hometown, Tyler, Wisconsin.

But Gina Santori is anything but thrilled to discover her
best friend has tricked her into sharing a room with
the man who broke her heart eight years ago....

And Delia Mayhew can hardly believe that she's
gotten herself locked in the Breakfast Inn Bed
basement with the sexiest man in America.

Then there's Rebecca Salter. She's turned up at the
Inn in her wedding gown. Minus her groom.

*Come home to Tyler for three delightful novellas
by three of your favorite authors: Kristine Rolofson,
Heather MacAllister and Jacqueline Diamond.*

HARLEQUIN®
Makes any time special ™